To anyone who ever wanted to spend just a little more time with Darcy and Elizabeth.

`

SPEECHLESS

JESSIE LEWIS

Quills & Quartos
PUBLISHING

Edited by Kristi Rawley and Sarah Pesce

Cover Design by Crowglass Design

ISBN

Ebook 978-1-951033-17-0

Paperback 978-1-951033-18-7

CONTENTS

The acknowledged
lovers talked and
laughed.
The unacknowledged
were silent.

Breathless

F ire. There was nothing else. It seared his chest, blistered his throat, and scorched his mind. Fear blinded him. His ears were deaf to all but a throbbing roar. He could not breathe; he could not move. He knew only fire—until oblivion extinguished even that.

PAIN ROUSED HIM AS MERCILESSLY AS IT HAD QUELLED HIM. FEROCIOUS, TERRIFYING pain unlike any he had ever known. An almighty thudding shook his mind inside his skull and beat its rage against his ribs. He fought to ease it, strained to fill the vacuum in his chest, but a sickening scrape arose, and no air penetrated his constricted throat. His lungs screamed their protest. He would have screamed also, had he any breath to spare.

He feared the pressure would rupture him somewhere and trembled at the thought. Waves of panic ebbed and flowed, the troughs of sweet numbness between them growing ever deeper, ever wider. The agony of hollow lungs became less than the torture of attempting to fill them. He ceased the attempt.

The rushing in his ears intensified, thrumming louder, murmuring, calling to him. Its words were unclear, but the tone of it—urgent, unyielding, familiar —caught him and held him just shy of obscurity. The harder he struggled, the more insistent grew the voice, compelling him to fight until, abruptly, icy air touched his burning lungs. Reflexively, he gulped for more.

"Short, shallow breaths. If you struggle, it will be worse."

The words kept their meaning greedily to themselves and left him to gasp in confusion and futility for another breath. He opened his mouth wide as though the sky might pour its contents into him. It did, and he choked on it—a gurgling, excruciating spasm that abraded his already fraying consciousness.

"You have been injured, sir! You must take shallower breaths."

He hauled leaden arms to claw at his throat and loosen whatever devil gripped him there, but his fingers discovered only more pain. Something took hold of his hands and moved them away. A gentle weight alit upon his breastbone.

"Concentrate on the rise and fall of your chest." The weight lifted. "A little up." A lighter pressure returned, forcing non-existent air from his lungs. "A little down. A little up. A little down. Dwell not on the pain, Mr Darcy. Think only of the rise and fall."

Mr Darcy, he thought. *I am he! I am he.*

When the weight lifted off his chest, he pushed his ribs after it, chasing the contact. And though his swollen gullet raged against the incursion, air trickled past in a wretched pretension to breath.

CONSCIOUSNESS CAME AND WENT, DELIVERING HIM IN AND OUT OF TORMENT. Whenever the darkness receded, so resumed his struggle. On and on, heartbeat after heartbeat, he battled to answer the furious demand for air. Now and then, he was buffeted by the world: a touch to his face, a limb rearranged, the muffled drone of words in his ear. Nothing obtruded sufficiently to rouse him to full awareness. All he knew was the effort to keep breathing.

If he lay sufficiently still, if he inhaled with adequate caution, he found he could manage it. Enough to stave off the myriad bursts of light that coalesced before his unseeing eyes with each missed breath. Whenever the pressure grew too great, he was recalled to the gentle but emphatic instruction to think of the rise and fall. The echo of it was all that remained. The voice itself had been absent for some time. The only sound to be heard was a hideous, wet rattle that seemed to come from inside his own head and coincided disconcertingly with his arduous respirations. Fear flooded him. It roiled in his gut, awaiting each moment stupefaction waned enough to promise a glimpse of lucidity, then arose to usurp all reason and tear up his composure.

There were no words of comfort left in the air, and what little connexion he retained to the world had become distinctly less human in nature. Absent were the touch of hands and warmth of breath upon his face. In their place were icy flicks of falling sleet, appalling coldness seeping into his bones, and unrelenting pain. Dread tightened its noose about his neck, forcing a crescendo in his rasping breaths. He was grievously injured—dying, mayhap—and he was alone. He cried out, though it made no sound. His mute scream only convulsed his tongue and churned his stomach.

An ephemeral glimmer of light seized him from the brink of despair. A faint arc of luminescence that swept by and fleetingly revealed a towering fortress of black trees and a thousand tumbling snowflakes. It passed over him again, and once again, before it ceased its beacon blink and became a constant glow. The trees reared up over him again. He heard shouting, briefly, before it receded beyond his ken and took the light with it. The trees shrank back into darkness. Something disturbed the snow by his shoulder; cold flecks spattered his cheek. A muted voice—"I am here!"—then no more.

DISTURBING, SHAPELESS DREAMS SLOUGHED AWAY TO REVEAL THE LOUD CLATTERING as a nightmare very much of the waking world. Would that his teeth not so forcefully bang together, nor his limbs so violently shake, for every tremor inflamed his agony, yet he was perishingly cold. Every arduous breath dragged icy air into his raw windpipe and could not have hurt more had he swallowed shards of glass. He drew ever smaller breaths, perfectly willing to forfeit consciousness in exchange for respite.

His little boat rocked and rocked until he feared it would tip him into the lake. His cousin, returned to boyhood, skimmed a pebble from the bank. It skipped across the water, growing larger the nearer it came, and hit Darcy in the chest, no longer a pebble but a boulder. It crushed him, squeezing the air from his lungs and forcing his eyes open.

There was movement, though no boat or lake, nor anything so reassuring as his cousin's youthful visage. Something beneath him did rock and sway. It matched the pitch and heave of his jagged breathing. He was not averse to it; it afforded something on which to concentrate other than fear and cold and hurt. Pitch and roll, inhale, exhale, pitch and roll, inhale, exhale.

A sudden lurch threw his arm sideways into mid-air. His head lolled violently in the same direction and pain exploded in his neck as it was wrenched askew. A cry he had no power to withhold slammed mutely against the obstruction in his gullet and all that escaped him was an agonised wheeze, followed by the wet clack of his ruined throat as he tried in vain to drag the lost air back in. His pulse raged in his ears.

God help me! He prayed and dared any deity to hear him over the cacophonous din of his breathing.

His arm was lifted back to his side. Something touched his face, gently rolled his head back into alignment, and held it there.

"Shallow breaths, sir. Concentrate on small, shallow breaths."

Darcy had no wish to concentrate on the torture of respiration. He attended, instead, to the heat of the hands that held his head steady and the familiar, feminine voice that assured him, against all obvious reason, that he would be well.

She was not usually so compliant. Her conversation was more commonly punctuated by enigmatic smirks and the challenge of a raised eyebrow. He regarded her, standing by the pianoforte, eyes flashing, and wondered if he might draw a rise were he to suggest they dance a reel. He could not ask, for the walls of Netherfield's drawing room wavered to such a degree as to impede his path to the instrument. The room creased and bunched itself out of existence. Elizabeth was tucked away within its folds and Darcy was cast adrift.

His cheeks were cold where the hands had been. There was clattering and banging, shouts, and a horse's whinny. There was dampness on his face, numbness in his feet, and agony everywhere else. He could make no sense of anything as he was jostled and tugged roughly about. The voice said something in a vexed tone, making it even more familiar. Then another, deeper voice was raised, and whatever Darcy lay upon was shoved violently forwards. The ground fell away, his arms slipped heavily from his sides to dangle over the abyss, and he gasped involuntarily, fearing he would likewise fall. Pain overwhelmed him and awareness fled.

In a vast, wall-less chamber, his old fencing instructor advanced towards him, arm and practice foil outstretched. Darcy had no foil of his own, nor the ability to move away. The instructor did not appear troubled by his student's disadvantage and grinned amiably as he slid the blade deep into Darcy's throat and out the other side. Light flickered all around, glinted briefly off the blade protruding from his neck, then flared blindingly and sent his dreams scattering.

Warmth stung his frozen skin. He forced his eyes open and squinted at the blurry mire of shapes looming over him. They pulled at his collar and poked at whatever lay beneath it that hurt so abominably. Darcy attempted to push them away, but his arms refused to comply. He shook his head—"No!"—then ground his teeth to stop from crying out as the movement tore his throat.

Every breath became harder won, every exhalation cost him a little more strength. Pain and air had become the same thing. The ground beneath him shifted again, and he was tossed about like flotsam on the ocean. He was at Ramsgate, in the sea. Wickham stood upon the quay, gripping Georgiana's wrist tightly and sneering down into the water. A chain about Darcy's ankle held him just below the surface. He could swim no higher, he could not reach his sister, he could not draw breath. He could do nothing but drown as the sound of the ocean filled his ears.

"Hush."

Something brushed against his forehead. He flinched from it, then from the bolt of agony that arced the length of his gullet.

"Hush. Calm yourself, sir. Try not to struggle—the worst is over. We shall not move you again."

He opened his eyes and blinked against the light. Elizabeth Bennet leant over him. It was a delusion of a different nature; less muted, less indistinct than the others. He liked it better.

"Mr Darcy? Can you hear me?"

To nod in the affirmative was a reflex not easily subdued, and he grimaced fiercely at yet another excruciating stab, then fought a rising swell of nausea as the grotesque clamour of his fractured breathing increased.

There was a touch to his hand. His fingers were pried open. Something to which he had not known he clung was tugged from his grasp and replaced with a warmer, gentler thing. Her hand. Why was she there?

"You must try not to give in to alarm, sir. I know you are in a great deal of pain, but you are safe now, and we shall find somebody to tend to you as soon as may be."

A darker blackness than merely the shadowy occlusion of closed eyes crept over him, and he could not fight it. He could only cling to Elizabeth, lest he be lost from the world entirely.

A More Familiar Delusion

Worse than the unrelenting sense of suffocation, worse even than the agony of whatever affliction gripped his throat, was the terrible thirst to which Darcy awoke. His tongue cleaved to his palate, his head pounded, and exhaustion pinned his arms to his sides. When he begged for water, his lips cracked and his tongue spasmed, but his plea remained unspoken, for no sound came from the parched wasteland of his mouth. He could hear the hoarse scrape of what he presumed was his breathing, a crackling that he supposed was a fire, the faint whistle of wind trespassing around an ill-fitted windowpane—but of his own voice, he heard not a croak.

Fear added its bite to the gnaw of thirst. What in God's name had happened to him? Fighting an upwelling of alarm, he forced his eyes open. He was in a chamber, the ceiling of which was yellowing and peppered with mildew. He could see the uppermost corner of a window from where he lay; it was glazed with diamonds of thick, distorted glass. The walls were painted a utilitarian shade of taupe. He did not know the place or why he was in it. The time of day eluded him, for the light was all wrong—grey and bright at the same time. He knew neither how he came to be there, nor how long ago he had arrived. All that was certain was that he hurt atrociously, though the reason for that was as shrouded in mystery as everything else, and the confusion of his mind terrified him almost as much as his physical suffering.

Thirst overshadowed everything, compelling him to lift his head in search of water. Excruciating pain drove him instantly back down, his eyes and jaw clenched shut and his mind awhirl, grasping futilely at wisps of memories that might—but did not—explain the feeling of being utterly spent, utterly broken. His neck was ablaze and there was something horribly unfamiliar about the way his head and shoulders were aligned—an unnatural rigidity betwixt the two that, when he reached up to touch it, felt numb, despite the monstrous pain. He dug his fingers into it, attempted to scratch away whatever was hurting him, but everything he did and everywhere he touched exacerbated the torture.

Something took hold of his hands. He recoiled from the contact, ripping free of its grip and shoving it away, fearful of anything touching him. The movement tightened the constriction about his throat. He tugged frantically at the collar of his shirt to relieve it, but again his hands were seized and drawn aside, this time more firmly. Somebody spoke, the words nebulous but the tone fretful. He was not alone! There was comfort in that—or at least, there would be, if only whoever it was would do something to relieve his torment.

He or she—*she*—said something else. He knew not what; he could not concentrate on anything beyond the all-consuming need for liquid. He begged for water and shuddered when his throat gave forth nothing but an arid wheeze and a flood of pain. He forced one eye open and mouthed his plea again at the silhouette bent over him.

For the briefest moment, Darcy forgot his thirst entirely as the achingly familiar apparition slid her hand beneath his head and lifted it slightly to meet the cup she held to his mouth.

"Sip it slowly, Mr Darcy. Your throat is wounded. You would not like to choke."

Then water trickled between his lips and all else became immaterial. He meant to sip, but need bade him gulp. His throat contracted, he bucked in agony, spluttered out most of the water and sucked the rest into his lungs.

"Calm yourself, sir. Breathe. 'Tis well. 'Tis well."

The composure of the voice was vastly at odds with the desperate situation. It steadied him until he ceased coughing. As did the hand that remained at the base of his neck. Somebody—the same woman, presumably—dabbed the water from his face. He strained to focus his gaze on her countenance, his eyes found hers, and his breath hitched, though nobody would have noticed amongst the already erratic clamour.

"Now *sip*," said Elizabeth Bennet—to all appearances the real one, not an apparition or a delusion or a dream.

What in blazes? Darcy wondered in bewilderment, for in his present condition, with his mind as empty as his lungs, he could think of no goodly explanation for her being there. He had not the strength to reflect upon it for long. Distracted by the cup that was back at his lips, he attended instead to assuaging his thirst, though the pain of swallowing and the effort not to gag made it impossible to take more than half a dozen sips. By the time Elizabeth laid his head gently back on the pillow and removed her hand, exhaustion had crept into Darcy's mind and settled heavily upon his limbs. His eyes were already closed.

He heard, and envied, the deep breath Elizabeth took. He heard her also as she let it out, slowly and a little shakily—and he heard her speak.

"Good. The only thing that could possibly make this situation worse would be if you were actually to die."

Sleep was upon him before her meaning could even begin to matter.

"COME, DARCY. I MUST HAVE YOU BREATHE. I HATE TO SEE YOU THRASHING ABOUT in this stupid manner."

Darcy opened his eyes. "Bingley?" The man standing over him in full evening dress did not look like his friend, but he sounded like him, and his cocked hat was placed the wrong way on his head, which seemed apropos. "What has happened to me?"

"Strangled, old fruit."

"Strangled? By whom?"

"A bear."

"What?"

Bingley was gone, however, and all was dark again.

Darcy sipped, for there was water upon his lips. "Who did this?" he begged, though this time he had no voice, and the question hurt to ask. He found he no longer cared. The means mattered little; that he was injured remained true whatever the cause. He sipped more water and prayed for everything to cease hurting. Never had he known pain that permeated even the deepest sleep. It did not relent even for a moment.

"Physician?" he begged—or attempted to. His numb lips misshaped the word, and the obstruction in his throat stole what was left of the plea. "*Poppy?*" he mouthed. "*Milk of the pop—*" He gave up, exhausted.

"I am sorry," a voice too feminine to be Bingley's said, "I have nothing to give you for the pain. Though—" A loud scrape muffled whatever words were spoken next, and the voice faded away. Time pulsed in Darcy's ears awhile. Pain throbbed in his neck, and he drifted helplessly in obscurity.

An icy touch at his throat awoke him. He flinched away from it, and then grimaced at the agony of so sudden a movement. He lifted a hand to identify the coldness that stung his skin but was pushed gently away.

"Pray, leave it a moment, Mr Darcy. 'Tis only snow."

He frowned, baffled, yet snow was a less threatening delusion than a murderous bear, and he had not the wits about him to query it. In any case, its icy burn had begun to affect a small but sublime reprieve from his torturous breathing—and he felt certain he knew that voice intimately enough to trust it.

"What has happened to me?"

He received no response. Somebody dabbed at the rivulets of melted snow that ran behind his ears and into his hair, but whomever did so gave him no answer. Perhaps it was another hallucination. He asked again. The fussing ceased.

"Forgive me, I cannot understand you. Could you move your lips more slowly?"

He thought he had spoken aloud. Though, he also imagined he had been talking to his sister and, it would now seem, this was not she. Was he losing his mind?

"*What happened?*" he mouthed slowly and pointed at his throat.

"You were kicked by a horse."

'It was more probable that he had been strangled by a bear. A man kicked in the neck by a horse would like as not be too dead to enquire about it, mutely or otherwise. Perhaps he *was* dead. He asked if it were so.

"I am sorry," came the answer after a pause. "I simply cannot understand what you are trying to say. Pray, rest for now. I can answer your questions when you are better recovered."

Dead people did not recover. With the snow at his neck now merely warm dampness and the constant scraping sound of his breathing showing no sign of abating, that seemed as much comfort as he was likely to find at the present moment. He released the last of the air in his chest and surrendered once again to darkness.

A Hopeless Business

T he room brightened, and though his head was thick with fog and his thoughts were scattered incoherently throughout the miasma, Darcy supposed he must be awake, for he became aware of the sound of somebody moving around and the quiet thrum of a voice not his own. The aching discomfort that had been his constant companion whilst he slept intensified with wakefulness. Everything from his scalp to the pit of his stomach throbbed sharply and breathing felt akin to sword-swallowing.

A rush of alarm brought with it the recollection that he was gravely wounded. *And in an unfamiliar place,* he thought, taking in his strange surroundings. The voice floated nearer, and a blurry figure leant over him, touched his forehead, then drifted off and was shut away behind what sounded like a closing door. *With* Elizabeth Bennet? *For crying out loud!*

Vague memories and half-dreams of his malaise returned to him in flashes, and though little of it was intelligible, the feeling of her having been there throughout, once acknowledged, could not be shaken. Was she tending to him? Aghast, but clumsy with fatigue, he assessed his state of dress with heavy hands. The totality of his attire consisted of a shirt and what felt to be his riding breeches. He closed his eyes, unsure whether to be horrified or relieved. Both, he supposed, for though the impropriety was mortifying, it could have been infinitely worse. In any case, the humiliation of Elizabeth's being there did not sting as much as the perverseness of it. For the better part of three months, Darcy had fought an insuperable fascination with the dark-eyed spitfire. Now he was not only back in her presence but apparently quite literally at her mercy. He doubted even his fanciful younger sister could invent a story to match such far-fetched happenstance.

Georgiana! At the remembrance of her, thither swept all his thoughts. A picture formed in his mind of her as a young child, reaching her hands up, pleading to be swung into his arms. Something swooped and plummeted in his gut at the prospect of her never again welcoming him home. How badly injured was he? His sister had lost too many relatives at too tender an age to suffer another grievance—and, at the present moment, with indistinct but terrible recollections of panic and suffocation plaguing him, his own death did not seem wholly improbable.

He raised his hands to explore his neck. A fleeting fear that he had lost all sensation there was replaced with the equally worrying discovery that it had been bandaged. Bandages meant an open wound. Trepidation weakened his arms; he lowered his hands so as not to see them shake and lay still, chasing his untethered thoughts as they dashed futilely from one matter to another, alighting on nothing long enough to properly comprehend it. Every question—from what had befallen him, to what would become of him, to how much dignity he had sacrificed to Elizabeth's care—led to the same murky impasse: there were no answers; he was helpless.

Alarm swarmed close to overflowing until a new vexation arose, and his thoughts took flight like a host of flies disturbed by the swat of a hand. He needed to relieve himself. There was a moment when fear might have turned to hysteria, for the situation could not have been more ridiculous; but Darcy was not naturally disposed to laugh at himself and instead, fear twisted into bitterness. He threw back the blanket and attempted to haul himself upright.

Sudden and horrific pain tore down his neck and pinned him to the bed. He pounded a fist on the mattress and gritted his teeth so hard his face hurt. Nobody came to his assistance—something by which he could not help but be further vexed. God knew he had no wish to be in this situation with Elizabeth Bennet of all people, but now that such had been forced upon him, he found that her *not* coming to his aid was even more objectionable. As soon as he felt able, he called to her and was dismayed when all that escaped his mouth was a watery scratching sound. He tried again but this time gagged on the utterance and almost lapsed insensate at the pain the attempt induced. Fear hammered in his veins. He could not speak! What the bloody hell was he to do with no voice?

Long moments filled with desolate predictions for his future passed, and no relief from agony arrived. Neither did Elizabeth. His perturbation increased tenfold at the possibility of having dreamt her up after all—for what did that say about the state of his mind? What it said about the state of his heart was something he was so averse to considering that he avoided it altogether by rolling onto his side, planting a hand on the bed and shoving himself roughly to sitting. The room simultaneously shrank and tilted as his vision blackened at the edges and his head swam vertiginously. He grabbed for the nightstand, knocked something off it that clanged loudly to the floor, and grimaced savagely to forestall the bellow he suspected would only choke him.

At length, his vision cleared, revealing an average-sized room, with too few windows to properly light the space, too much furniture to let in what little light there was, and no Elizabeth. He was not alone though. Over the scrape and crackle of his breathing, he could hear the faint din of conversation creeping up through the floorboards. He stared at them, beneath his feet, attempting to think how best to gain somebody's attention through the thick oak, but his addled thoughts refused to attend to the problem. The roar of pain in his ears worsened by the moment, suffocating every thought that lingered too long. His feet were cold—the rest of him was not—a fire burned in the hearth—his neck hurt—his boots stood in the corner of the room at right angles to each other—his head hurt—there was only one bed—a chamber pot protruded from under it. At last—an observation of some actual use!

With as little movement to his upper body as possible, Darcy hooked a foot behind the pot, slid it into position, used it without standing up, and shoved it back beneath the bed with his heel. Confusion trespassed ever farther over his awareness. Every movement he made, every moment he remained upright, every breath for which he fought increased the agony in his neck and his desperation to find relief. He grabbed hold of the nightstand with both hands and would have heaved himself to his feet had the door not opened, and Elizabeth cried out in alarm.

"Sir! What in the world are you doing?" She dropped whatever had been in her arms and hastened to his side. "This is madness! Pray, get back into bed!"

Madness was Elizabeth Bennet clutching at his arms through naught but his shirt sleeves and demanding that he go anywhere near a bed, and Darcy had no intention of following that path. This delusion could go to hell and take all such lunacy with it. He hauled himself up.

"Upon my word, you cannot be seri—" She finished with a grunt as she took the entirety of his toppling weight and redirected it with a shove towards the bed, onto which Darcy collapsed just as blackness rose up to claim him.

HE DID NOT FEEL MUCH RESTED WHEN PAIN NEXT ROUSED HIM. UNSURE HOW LONG he had slept, he awoke to an increasingly familiar succession of astonishment, delight, and horror upon realising that he was trapped in singularly close quarters with Elizabeth Bennet. He heard her before he saw her, speaking to herself as she walked about the room. Nay, not herself, him.

"...have torn up enough cloth to make do. 'Tis clean, at least." She came into sight and busied herself unloading the items in her arms onto a nearby table. "Mr Timmins was good enough to give me some brandy, though I expect he will add it to our account." She picked up the ewer and poured steaming water into a bowl. "I told him it was to cleanse the wound, but if you could manage to swallow some, it might dim the pain. Though, I daresay your pain would be infinitely less had you not determined to throw yourself about the room like that."

Darcy's neck spasmed as the memory of standing—and falling—resurfaced with a jolt. That he had forgotten in so short a space of time, despite his discomfort having been significantly worse upon waking, made him excessively uneasy. Never had he been so addled, so incapable of recalling what was happening to him from one moment to the next. His heart increased its pace until he could ignore it no longer, and though he would more commonly be able to reason away such feelings of anxiety, his mind would not comply. Every bit of logic at which he grasped wafted away like smoke sucked from the air by an opening door. He reached instead for something more tangible, tapping Elizabeth's arm to gain her attention, but he recoiled when she shrieked and spilled water all over the nightstand.

"I thought you were asleep, sir! You made no sound!"

He grimaced and mouthed, *"I cannot speak."* The admission hastened his heartbeat further still.

Elizabeth set the ewer down and leant to peer more closely at him. "You cannot speak?"

Darcy shook his head and cursed himself for doing it when the skin upon his neck felt as though it tore afresh.

"At all?"

"No!" he said in exasperation—except he did not say it, he only gagged on the attempt and snarled in frustration.

"Perhaps you ought not to attempt to say anything for now," Elizabeth said, frowning. "I daresay I shall scarcely notice the difference, and your voice will no doubt return more quickly if you allow your throat to heal first."

"What has happened to my throat?" he mouthed urgently, wild to comprehend why he had no voice.

She pulled an apologetic face and shook her head. "Could you say the words more slowly? I cannot understand you."

He held out both hands in as close an approximation to a shrug as he could manage without moving his shoulders and mouthed, *"What happened?"*

Elizabeth frowned at his lips, silently mimicking their movements with her own as she attempted to comprehend his meaning. When she did, she transferred her frown to his eyes. "You do not remember?"

Darcy forgot not to shake his head and winced at another wave of pain.

"Forgive me. No more yes or no questions. Mr Darcy, you have been kicked by a horse."

God help him, he was still delusional! *"What?"* he mouthed, fierce despite his muteness, for his incomprehension terrified him. *"How can that be?"*

"You were attempting to cut it free."

He continued to look at her, still none the wiser.

She took a deep breath, then exhaled and shook her head decisively. "It is not a brief explanation. Allow me to attend to your wound before this water cools, else I shall have to heat more. After that, I shall explain everything."

Darcy would have groaned had he been able, for everything Elizabeth said confused him more. Why was she heating her own water? Where were they that there were no servants to even boil a kettle? Why, in God's name, were either of them there?

"*Attend to my wound?*" he repeated stupidly.

"I need to change the bandages, or it will fester."

"*No!*" Darcy was not sure to what he was objecting; *anything* touching the monstrous rawness at his neck, it being Elizabeth who would do so, or simply having been injured in the first place. His breathing had grown too fast; it was hurting his throat and making an unearthly sound.

"No?" Elizabeth repeated, not unkindly but with a hint of impatience. "Mr Darcy, I am aware that you are very unwell, but please try to understand me. Your wound is unstitched. It was in need of redressing even before your ill-advised attempt to get out of bed. Now, I should say it is essential."

The thrum of alarm pulsed mercilessly in Darcy's ears. A wound severe enough to require stitching, but which had not been—what manner of hell *was* this?

"Should you like some brandy before I begin?"

He blinked her countenance back into focus. He had meant to say something of it being too much to ask that she perform the task, but befogged with pain, his mind had wandered again, and she had taken his silence for consent. Unable to think of a sensible reason to refuse, he nodded yes to the brandy, quailed as pain ignited under his chin, opened his mouth to cry out, choked before any sound escaped and mouthed a thoroughly uncivil imprecation.

Elizabeth raised both eyebrows, but if she recognised his incivility, she was good enough not to mention it, and said instead, "We must devise a better way to communicate. One that does not require you to nod or shake your head. Perhaps you could blink once for yes and twice for no?"

A simple solution—he blinked once.

"No?" she replied dubiously.

He frowned and blinked once again.

"Yes? Stop blinking!"

He lifted his hands in another shrug.

"Just blink once if you agree," Elizabeth said again, very slowly, as though speaking to a child.

Doing his best to conceal his exasperation, Darcy squeezed his eyes closed overlong, then opened them again—one unmistakable blink.

Elizabeth smirked. "You keep blinking again after you have said yes."

Panic and pain melted away as Darcy beheld her expression. It felt an awfully long time that he been longing to see her eyes gleam with mirth in that manner. He reeled at the intensity with which he felt the effect, having thought to have reasoned himself out of any susceptibility to her charms weeks ago.

"There is no need to look so cross. You cannot help blinking. It is evidently not a sound suggestion. Why not extend your forefinger to say no?"

Darcy did as she suggested.

"Aye, that works well enough. I cannot mistake you when you look so much as though you are scolding me. And for yes, you could—"

He dipped his extended finger to touch the back of his other hand.

"That will do well enough." She twisted away to collect something from the table. "Now, to avoid the necessity for any more answers of any sort, I intend to spoon this brandy into you until you stop glowering at me." She held the bottle up to the window and squinted at it. "I do hope we have enough."

He smiled at her teasing, but stopped again directly, for he had no intention of worsening his plight or undoing weeks of struggles by being drawn back in at the very first hint of Elizabeth's playfulness.

DARCY SPLUTTERED AND CHOKED DOWN AS MUCH BRANDY AS HE COULD THEN pushed away the next spoonful Elizabeth brought to his lips. His pain had not much abated and certainly not enough to compensate for the sting of attempting to swallow the acrid swill. God, but he was tired!

"Are you ready?" Elizabeth enquired then immediately added, "Do not nod! I ought not to have asked. You will just have to accustom yourself to being told what to do." He heard her dip something in the water and wring it out. "It will make a nice change from you directing everybody else's affairs."

He frowned over her meaning until something hot touched his throat and crawled in every direction over his skin. He gasped—a painful and noisy affair —and attempted to pull away from it but succeeded only in hurting himself more.

"I know it pains you," Elizabeth said, "but I must soak these bandages, or I fear I will reopen whatever has begun to heal when I take them off."

He looked in dismay at the bloodied cloth in her hand.

She looked from him to it and back. "I shall not lie to you, sir—there was a good deal of blood."

He wondered vaguely whether having bled a lot would account for the tingling warmth that was presently blooming in his fingers and toes. Elizabeth reapplied the damp cloth, and the crawling heat returned as water soaked into the bandages. Her brow contracted as she applied herself to the task, and her gaze flicked frequently to his as though to gauge his condition. Being even less certain of that than she, Darcy was able to offer nothing by way of encouragement and could only watch her silently as she worked.

Her hair was different, pinned simply and escaping from its confines in a dozen places. One wisp, hanging by her temple, bounced hypnotically each time she leant over him. Her touch was soporific in its gentleness. Every point at which his distress grew too great, she paused and waited for him to recover himself, her gaze steady and her smile encouraging. He had lied to himself;

she was far prettier than his memory had allowed her to be. When she wiped her brow with the back of her hand and inadvertently smeared his blood across her face, he groaned inwardly. This was too gruesome a task for so respectable and genteel a woman. *"Why you?"*

He had meant to mutter it only to himself, forgetting Elizabeth was poised to read his lips, and he started when she said, heatedly, "There is nobody else! I suppose you would rather avoid the indignity, but the alternative is that I leave you to moulder, perchance to die, and I refuse to believe there is not somebody, *somewhere* in the world, who would care if you did."

She had mistaken him, of course, but he was diverted by her feisty retort, so reminiscent of their every exchange at Netherfield. He extended his forefinger to contradict her and gave the silent explanation, *"That was not my meaning."* He could easily perceive she had not managed to catch his words, and he tried again. *"I am sorry for you."* On a whim, he reached up and wiped the blood from her forehead with his shirt cuff. He pointed at her and mouthed, *"Lovely."* Then he pointed at his injury and mouthed, *"Not lovely."*

She pulled a sceptical face and pointed at him. "Drunk."

He could not help but laugh and, hence, gag. He sucked in a slow, rasping breath and held it until the risk of coughing, sniggering, or indeed suffocating passed. When it had, he gestured for her to continue and squeezed his eyes closed in readiness. He began to suspect she might be right when the world began to spin in slow, nauseating revolutions. Still, he supposed that above four-and-twenty hours without food would leave a man susceptible to two or three dozen spoonfuls of cheap alcohol. He opened his eyes and stared at the ceiling. The patches of mildew swirled and bloomed into patterns. One was shaped just like a pineapple.

"Mr Darcy? I have finished washing it. Sir? Are you well?"

He rolled his head back to squint at Elizabeth but was unsure how to answer. He was in a vast amount of pain, devilishly confused, prodigiously drunk, and very much enamoured of the woman responsible for most of these misfortunes. He wrinkled his nose in ambivalence.

Elizabeth's mouth twitched, and her eyes shone in that way they always did when something diverted her. "A little less brandy next time, perhaps."

"I would prefer less horse."

It took Elizabeth a moment of studying his lips before she comprehended him. Her delayed burst of laughter surprised and delighted him, though he was rather distracted when she abruptly split in two, and each version of her drifted a foot apart from the other before snapping back to not quite line up. Both of her smiles were sublime.

"Perhaps I ought to give you nothing *but* brandy if we are to survive this predicament. Inebriation suits you rather better than hubris." She selected a strip of clean cloth from the table, explaining to him as she did that she would now re-dress his wound.

Darcy held up a hand to forestall her and mouthed, *"Mirror?"*

She hesitated, evidently unwilling to comply.

Naturally, that begged the question, *"Bad?"*

She held his gaze and replied gently but without preamble, "Yes, it is quite bad."

"Show me?"

"Why not wait until it is better healed? There is no advantage in distressing yourself."

"You are not distressed."

She frowned over his words, repeating them herself until they were familiar enough to recognise. "I am...not...distre— 'Tis not my throat!"

He had forgotten her obstinacy, though he ought not to have done, for he was well acquainted with it. The dogged manner in which she had harried him at Bingley's ball for details of his dispute with Wickham, with the evident purpose of exonerating the fiend, had haunted him for many weeks now. Nevertheless, her obduracy was no match for the recalcitrance of a drunkard. He fixed her in his gaze and persisted, mouthing, *"I would see."*

Elizabeth sighed and squared her shoulders. "As you wish." She left his side and returned with a modestly sized table mirror that had a spider's web of cracks spreading out from one shattered corner. She hefted it onto her forearm for support and obligingly held it above him with both hands.

Never had Darcy beheld such a sobering sight. His heart pounded and his head cleared of fog—and pretty much all else—as he stared in horror at his reflection. A day's worth at least of beard covered his jaw, but the rest of his face was pallid and drawn. His throat was bruised indigo and swollen to well beneath the collar of his shirt. A peculiarly straight laceration ran from under the right of his chin to the hollow above his collar bone. With his every rasping breath, the whole ruinous mess shifted and wept. He understood now why he could scarcely breathe and no longer wondered at the torment of every trifling movement of his head. He was fortunate to be alive. How long he would remain so with such an injury was not something on which he should like to wager.

"It ought to be stitched, but there is no one to do it. The best I can do is hold it closed with bandages." The impatience had gone from Elizabeth's voice; her tone was all compassion, though it scarcely penetrated Darcy's dismay. "Be reassured, at least, that your collar prevented any dirt from getting into the wound. As long as we keep it clean, and you do not try to overexert yourself again, I see no reason why it should not heal well enough."

She said nothing about the recovery of his voice, though Darcy supposed it wisest to concern himself with surviving over and above being able to talk about it. Nevertheless, he could not help but stare at the wreckage of his neck and attempt to guess where, exactly, his vocal cords might be located and thereby how badly damaged they might be. The longer he stared, the greater grew his revulsion. It was a relief when Elizabeth lowered the mirror to the floor. He mouthed his thanks.

"It is well, sir. It is not as though I am going anywhere. Besides, I spoke true when I said I was concerned for those who care for you. I could not bear the thought of Miss Darcy losing her brother on account of his trying to help me."

Darcy frowned in puzzlement; the fog was returning. *"Help you?"*

"Why, yes." She leant over him with a clean linen with which to bind his neck. He tried in earnest to listen to what she said, but her voice was so dulcet and his mind so hazy that her words all ran into one another. His eyelids grew too heavy to keep open and not even the pain of having his wound pulled closed with bandages could prevent him slipping into the encroaching torpor.

No Less Resentment than Despair

W hen next he awoke, Darcy recalled much more much sooner. Regrettably, all the unpleasant recollections—the pain, the exhaustion, the fear, the pounding legacy of too much cheap brandy— loomed large, and the only one of his remembrances he wished were there was not. He called to her but was still unable to make a sound, and the attempt pained him severely. He clawed at the bedsheets as though he could draw her nearer by gathering the room towards him. Elizabeth did not come.

Though it was tempting to give in to alarm, Darcy retained grasp enough on his reason to recognise it would achieve naught. Besides, had she not remarked that she was going nowhere? He indulged in the heartening assurance that she must be nearby and allowed himself a deep, albeit careful, sigh of relief. He followed it immediately with a sneer of disdain. But a few days ago, he had been assured of a complete triumph over his errant feelings for Elizabeth Bennet. All but banished from his thoughts, she had been relegated to a troublesome memory. Would he now succumb to panic at the mere prospect of her absence? The very idea was absurd. *Anybody's* assistance at the present time would be equally valuable, and it mattered not whether it were Elizabeth, a total stranger, or the Queen-of-blasted-Sheba.

He resolutely ignored the little jolt in his chest when the door opened and neither the Queen of Sheba nor a total stranger entered the room.

"You are awake," Elizabeth remarked. She looked tired—an observation that stirred all manner of concern in Darcy's mind, though he knew not what he could do about it. "I have brought you some broth," she told him, setting a steaming tankard and spoon on the table. "You will not begin to improve until you regain some strength."

At the mention and then the smell of food, Darcy's stomach spasmed violently in revenge for having been so long neglected. He mouthed his thanks and attempted to haul himself into a more upright position in readiness. He had expected it to hurt; he had not expected to be unable to do it. The flesh of his neck twisted sickeningly, and his arms trembled and gave way before he had pulled himself more than a few inches up the bed.

"I rest my case," Elizabeth said with a satirical glance. "But Heaven forfend you should listen to me."

"I meant not to disregard you," Darcy mouthed, glad of his muteness for the first time, for had he spoken, his voice might have betrayed the extent of his alarm. *"I thought I could sit up. I managed it this morning."*

Elizabeth shook her head. "I have no idea what you just said, but I shall save us both the trouble of your repeating it and assume it was ill-tempered."

He had not the energy to smile at her teasing. Indeed, he scarcely had the energy to be surprised when she lifted one knee onto the edge of the bed and knelt over him with her hands out.

"Give me your arms, Mr Darcy."

He stared at her, wondering whether he had fallen asleep again—or was, perhaps, still drunk.

"Pray, help me, if you would. I cannot lift you on my own. If you allow me to pull you forward, then I can prop you up with another pillow, so you can eat."

He did as she bid, clenching his jaw against the pain as she tugged him forward. He saw the moment she realised he was hurting. Her eyes widened, and she winced as though she felt it herself. To his astonishment, she let go of one of his arms and slid her hand behind his head to support it as she pulled him forward. He flinched when her fingers found something else that hurt—an excessively sore spot at the side of his head—but he forgot it when Elizabeth reached around him to place the extra pillow before gently laying him back down.

"Is that comfortable?" she enquired.

Darcy had never been less comfortable in his life, but his proximity to Elizabeth, her arms around him and her fingers in his hair, had driven most rational thought from his mind. He dazedly made the gesture for yes and mouthed a silent thank you.

"Hold on to your thanks for now," she replied with a half-hearted smile. "You have not yet tasted this broth." She withdrew to fetch it, and while she was turned away, Darcy explored the back of his head with his fingers. There was a lump behind his ear, which, though not nearly as painful as his neck, was nevertheless disconcerting in size and tenderness.

"You have a lump there," Elizabeth said, returning with the broth.

"So it would seem."

"I think you hit your head when you were knocked backwards."

Darcy lowered his hand and resolved not to examine any other parts of himself lest he discover any further injuries, for he had more than sufficient already.

With a sympathetic smile, Elizabeth arranged herself on the edge of the bed with the tankard and spoon, dipped one into the other and held it out for Darcy to sup. He gently wrapped his hand around hers and guided her to empty the spoon back into the tankard, which he then took from her grasp. The ignominy of being observed by Elizabeth in so indecent and feeble a state was outside of enough without adding to it by consenting to be fed like an infant.

He pointed at himself and mouthed, "*I shall do it.*"

Elizabeth graciously inclined her head and removed from the bed to sit in a nearby chair. Darcy wished she would not watch him, for though he could get the spoon to his mouth, he was unable to hold his head at an angle sufficient to prevent rivulets of broth running from it into his new beard—but such vanity was soon forgotten. He managed the first few mouthfuls without event but gagged on the third and suffered such a virulent fit of agonising paroxysms as drew Elizabeth from her chair in alarm.

"Oh my goodness! Calm yourself, or you will choke!" She took the tankard from him and set it aside then returned to sitting on the edge of the bed. Darcy had his hands to his throat, desperate for some way to allay the spasms, and she took hold of them, pulled them away from his neck, and held them. "Try to relax, sir. You are very rigid. I can see it is making it worse."

It was, but he knew not what he could do about it. Each time he attempted to stifle a convulsion, another rose up to strangle him, until he coughed suddenly and violently, and blood spattered both their hands. The rasp of him frantically filling his lungs was loud, but still did not completely mask Elizabeth's horrified gasp. He shared her dismay and stared aghast at the peppering of bright red across the bed, wondering very seriously whether he would die in this room.

"Oh."

The interjection was almost inaudible, but the tremble in Elizabeth's voice as she uttered it was unmistakable. Darcy looked up. He had never seen her frightened. She looked less assured, more innocent than ever she had before. It roused him from his own misery and directed his concern in the proper direction. After a few steadying, if cacophonous, breaths, he used the corner of the blanket to wipe the blood from her hands. "*Forgive me.*"

She shook her head lightly. "No, no—there is no need to apologise. Can you breathe now? Are you well?"

"*I am.*" Though he was certain she had understood his few words, she did not appear much reassured, and he felt obliged to substantiate them with actions. Thus, though it was the very last thing he wished to do, Darcy reached for the tankard and brought another spoonful of broth to his lips. Swallowing hurt like the devil, and it took all his strength of will not to gag on this, or the next several mouthfuls. When he could stomach no more, he returned the broth to the nightstand and sought Elizabeth's gaze. *"Better going in than coming out."*

Why he had thought such a crude remark would reassure her he knew not, and he cringed inwardly until Elizabeth deduced what he had mouthed, gave him a look of astonished incredulity, and burst out laughing. Then he could have forgiven himself a hundred obscenities for the simple pleasure of seeing the fear driven from her eyes.

"I am glad you approve," she said, "for that is the best for which you can hope at the present time. There is little else available. Not that you would be able to swallow at any rate."

And so on to serious matters. *"Will you tell me where we are?"* Darcy enquired mutely. *"And what has happened?"*

She watched his lips but shook her head apologetically. "I do not—"

"Pen?" Darcy mimed the act of writing as he asked.

"Oh, a pen! Of course! One moment." Elizabeth stood up from the bed with haste, and Darcy flinched at the pain of being jostled against the pillows. She left the room via a door he had not previously noticed—an adjoining bedchamber, he presumed, when she returned from it with a pen, a pot of ink, and a handful of papers.

"Mrs Ormerod was good enough to lend me these. Here." She handed him the whole stack of paper. "If you take it all, it ought to be a sturdy enough surface."

Darcy had no idea who Mrs Ormerod might be, but he let it pass. He had only one pen and limited strength and would have to settle for a single question at a time. He dipped the pen in the ink Elizabeth held out for the purpose and wrote as best he could in his present attitude,

Where are we?

He held it up for her to read.

She frowned. "You do not recall any of what I told you this morning?" More urgently, she added, "Use your hands to answer!"

Darcy smiled gratefully for the timely reminder and extended his forefinger rather than shake his head.

Elizabeth pulled a wry face. "I did wonder if you had heard me."

He scribbled another quick note.

Forgive me. I have been excessively fatigued.

He held it up again.

"'Tis well, sir," she assured him after reading it. "You have been very seriously injured. It is not surprising you have been muddled. We are at an inn called The Dancing Bear, near Spencer's Cross. Do you know it?"

Darcy shook his head and cursed silently, no less from the pain than exasperation at having done so yet again.

"My apologies," Elizabeth said. "Asking questions is a difficult habit to unlearn. Spencer's Cross is a small village a short distance south of here. Beech Hill, I understand, is a little farther, and to the east." She stopped and seemed to be waiting for him to respond. He indicated that he required more ink, then wrote,

Why are we here?

This time, before he could hold it up for her to read, she shuffled her chair closer to the bed and leant forward to read it where it was in his lap. Darcy smirked at her impatience at first, then sobered as her closeness threatened to affect him in ways he prodigiously wished it would not.

"I cannot say what *you* were doing in this part of the world," she said, straightening to look at him again. She put the ink pot on the nightstand and clasped her hands together on the edge of the bed. "*I* was travelling to London to see my sister Jane. She has been staying there with my aunt and uncle since Christmas."

Two things happened while Elizabeth said this: her expression grew disconcertingly steely, and Darcy's stomach clenched with something disagreeably like guilt. Could Elizabeth be aware he had concealed her sister's presence in Town from Bingley? Surely not—and what ought it to matter if she were? He kept his expression neutral and waited for her to continue.

"Regrettably, we were caught short by the weather en route and forced to divert onto a road with more cover overhead."

Darcy baulked as that part of his own memory resurfaced with mortifying clarity. He had been at St Albans, visiting friends. Returning to London ought to have taken a matter of hours—a direct carriage ride down the Great North Road. And so it might have been, were it not for the moment of madness that came upon him as he readied himself on the morning of his departure.

He could picture in his mind's eye the colour that arose in his cheeks as he stood before his dressing mirror, torturing himself with the knowledge that St Albans was but ten miles from Meryton. Ten miles from the town to where often walked the woman he had not seen since he danced with her at Bingley's ball last November. Ten miles from the woman who had plagued almost every one of his waking thoughts—and as sure as the devil every *single* dream—since. Ten miles from the woman whose equal he had yet to find anywhere in the whole of his acquaintance. He had fought long and hard to relinquish his attachment and would not seek her out by design—but the temptation of a serendipitous encounter had proved too much to resist. He had sent his man home in the carriage and set out on horseback along the alternative route back to London, via Meryton.

No such encounter had occurred—at least, not that he recalled. The snow had started to fall whilst his horse rested at one of Meryton's coaching inns and begun to settle by the time he set out again towards Ermine Street. A snowbound road and a diversion down an easier path both rang faint bells amongst his otherwise hazy memories of the rest of that day.

He looked away to the darkest corner of the room, attempting to conceal the disdain curling his lip, for it was not meant for Elizabeth. He was never impetuous. *Bingley* was the impulsive one, forever landing himself in awkward scrapes as a consequence of caprice. Darcy had made it the study of his life to always act with purpose and forethought—and so he had achieved until Elizabeth waltzed into his world and made a reckless fool of him. And look where his newfound imprudence had led! At worst he was a dead man, at best he was a mute, and either way he was marooned with the one woman whom he was damned if he could resist but whom duty forbade him from ever having!

"There *was* less snow on the other road," Elizabeth continued, "but, it tran-spired, more ice. I do not know precisely how it happened, but our carriage overturned."

Darcy's heart gave a great thud, and he whipped his gaze back to hers, ignoring the searing pain in his neck. She looked pained but composed, and her aplomb shamed him far more than a display of hysteria would have. She had given no hint of having suffered any misfortune, and so preoccupied with his own accident had he been that it never occurred to him she might also have been injured. "*Good God!*" he mouthed, "*Were you hurt?*"

She watched him say the words but struggled to understand, no doubt due to the urgency with which they were said. He snatched up the pen and scratched out the enquiry on paper.

"Oh, nothing broken," she replied dismissively. "But Perkins, my uncle's man, he—" She stopped speaking abruptly and looked at her hands. When she spoke again, her tone was sombre, and she did not look up. "He was travelling with me in the carriage due to the cold, and when it began to swerve, he leant out of the window to call to the driver and—that is when it happened. I believe he broke his neck."

"*Dear God!*" Darcy waited for her to glance up and mouthed clearly, "*I am very sorry.*"

"As am I," she replied quietly. "I barely knew him, but I know my uncle thought very well of him, and I am sure the Perkins family will be devastated. Such a needless tragedy. My uncle or my father will have to compensate them —and buy a new carriage—and all because I desired to go to London a fort-night early! Had I only waited and gone when I had planned to, it would all have been avoided."

Darcy's first instinct was to pull her into his arms and whisper his assur-ances until she denounced all notion of blame. His second was to push such foolish wishes from his mind and indicate mutely for more ink. He waited for Elizabeth to hold it out to him, dipped his pen, and wrote,

I am grieved that you had to witness such a thing.

She read it and gave him a wry smile. "It was horrible, I shall not deny it, though I am not the sort to faint away in the face of real life, sir. Which is fortunate, given what happened next." She looked pointedly at him and took a deep breath before elaborating. "Rogers, the driver, freed one of the horses. The other was trapped somehow in the harness, and it was…screaming. I have never heard a horse make such a noise. He could not get to it, I could not get to him, for the carriage door would not open properly. And then *you* appeared."

Darcy vaguely remembered the sound of a horse screaming—and a woman, who must have been Elizabeth. The image of her trapped in an overturned carriage with a dead man, crying for help, raised the hairs on his arms.

"Once I climbed out, I saw you both working to free the horse. Rogers was holding up the crossbar, and you were trying to untether the harness under the horse's belly, and it was thrashing about and…and it just…it all happened so quickly I cannot say with certainty, but I believe it caught you in the throat with its foreleg or some part of the traces or I know not what! But you sort of"—she moved both hands in parallel through the air, watching the space between them as though envisioning him moving with them—"flew backwards and landed in the snow." She looked up to meet his eyes. "I thought you must be dead too, but you were not."

Darcy felt slightly nauseous, though whether at the grisly scene Elizabeth depicted or the snatches of looming trees, falling snow, and suffocation that nagged him to remember them, he could not tell.

"Do you recall any of this?"

He wrote his answer slowly, feeling somewhat dazed.

Some of it.

After a moment's thought, he added,

I recall being unable to breathe.

"You could not—not properly. I thought you would stop at every moment, but, well, here you are. Rogers would not leave me alone on the road, so I did what I could to keep you warm and left with him to find help. We took your horse—I hope you do not mind. At least he is safe in the stables here now."

Darcy smiled his acquiescence. Fine beast though it was, his horse was the least of his concerns.

"This was the nearest inhabited place. One of the guests, Mr Stratton, lent us his carriage and sent his man with us to help carry you. The innkeeper sent his nephew as well."

Darcy reached for the ink. Elizabeth waited in silence for him to write.

You returned with them?

She drew back, her expression turned cold. "Yes, I did. I suppose it would have been more ladylike to remain here and let the men fetch you—and it certainly would have been less troublesome—but in all honesty, it did not occur to me. We may not be the best of friends, Mr Darcy, but we are well enough acquainted that I could not countenance leaving you to the mercy of strangers. Not in this state."

Darcy not only extended his finger to object but held it up between them to ensure she saw it. When he had her attention, he wrote,

I do not mean to disapprove. I am only surprised—and grateful!

"Oh, I see." Elizabeth deflated somewhat, though she lost none of the fire from her eyes. She wrapped her hands around the worn ends of the arms of her chair and rubbed them absentmindedly as though wishing to direct her vexation somewhere, if not at him.

Darcy would have taken more time to assure her of his admiration for her courage and compassion were he not so close to exhaustion. The pain in his neck had grown nigh unbearable, his breathing had taken on a quality not dissimilar to the din of a sawmill, and his ears rang from the heaviness of the congestion in his head. He opted to glean more answers over offering compliments before sleep reclaimed him.

Then?

"There is not much more to tell," Elizabeth replied with a small shrug. "We brought you back here, and here we are still."

Darcy used the last of the ink on the pen to enquire,

Why?

Elizabeth leant forward to read it and gave a small scornful scoff before she sat back and said with no little disdain, "We are snowed in."

He raised a dubious eyebrow.

"There is no need to look at me in that manner, sir. I am well aware of the absurdity of the situation. There could not be two people with so little desire to be in the same place, yet here we are, detained together in the most intimate circumstances by a snowdrift. You really could not make it up."

Darcy kept watching her. She was right; he could think of little worse than being trapped in a confined space with the woman who tested his restraint more than any he had ever met. The possibility that she should feel similarly about him sparked the same flickering tightness in his chest that had assailed him constantly during his stay in Hertfordshire last autumn. Resolving to disregard it, he held the pen out for more ink, his arm almost too heavy to lift clear of the bed.

Who else is here?

Elizabeth looked displeased with the question. "I assure you, were any of the other guests willing or able to assist, I should hardly refuse, but there is nobody."

Darcy closed his eyes briefly. Lovely she may be, but he wished Elizabeth were not quite so determined to always misunderstand him. Why she should always assume he meant to upbraid her, God only knew. Perhaps because her mother did naught else, she had grown used to defending herself? With leaden fingers, he scrawled an almost illegible explanation.

Would know you are safe.

She appeared somewhat puzzled by this. "I beg your pardon, sir. I thought… Never mind. 'Tis a small inn, run by the owner, Mr Timmins, and his nephew, Master John. He informs me his sister usually lives here also, but she has not been able to return from a visit to her mother since the snow began. The other guests are Mr and Mrs Ormerod, Lieutenant Carver—"

The pen fell from Darcy's hand. He reached after it instinctively, jarred his neck, and flung himself back onto the pillows only to receive another burst of pain from the lump on his head. He held himself rigid, exasperated by debility and wheezing in agony.

Elizabeth retrieved the pen from the floor and removed the paper from his lap. "I am perfectly safe, Mr Darcy," she said softly. "There are eight people here other than you and me, and they have all been exceedingly kind. You need not concern yourself for my well-being."

Darcy smiled weakly but earnestly. *"Good."*

Without further word, Elizabeth once more knelt on the edge of the bed and held out her arms for him. He accepted her help and allowed himself to be pulled forward. Rather than removing the extra pillow, however, she surprised him by letting go of his arms, crouching to the floor and sliding the chamber pot from beneath the bed. Had Darcy been any more alert, he would have been better able to express the extent of his mortification. As it was, all he could manage was a level stare and a vaguely disbelieving look.

"As I told you," she said, "I am not one to shy from real life. You need my help to sit up—therefore, either I help you, or, well—" A simple shrug said all that was needed. "I shall send Master John up presently to fetch it." She indicated the offending article with a nod. Then she reached to move the extra pillow from behind him, gave him a small smile, and left the room.

Darcy rubbed his face with both hands. Then he grabbed the nightstand as he had earlier in the day, though he stopped short of attempting to pull himself to his feet, forced to acknowledge that he could not even sit up unaided, let alone stand—had done himself untold damage attempting it once already. And what was the point in any case? They were snowed in. Even were he able to walk, he would get no farther than the front door. He had not the slightest hope of being rescued, for he had informed nobody of his intention to travel this way. He let go of the nightstand and struck it forcefully with his fist. The movement jarred his neck, and he bared his teeth in pain and vexation.

How had it come to this? The last few years had brought him more than his share of misfortunes, but never had he thought to end up bloodied and enfeebled in a dilapidated hovel with Elizabeth Bennet positioning a pot at his feet in which for him to piss. To think, when they had stayed under the same roof at Netherfield, he had considered the struggle to suppress his feelings for her the worst form of torture! He struck the nightstand again, twice, and welcomed the pain it occasioned, for he was helpless in every other respect; he may as well triumph in his despair.

Why her? He railed to himself. Why, of all the strangers in the country, must it be she with whom Fate had abandoned him in this state? And, worse than her seeing him dishevelled and unshaven, worse than his vomiting blood over her, worse than her bandaging his grotesque injury or setting the damned pot at his feet, was that she did it *all* with such captivating élan. He barely had the strength to see straight; how was he ever to find the strength to resist her? Even if he escaped this place alive, which he was entirely unconvinced he would do, he would never leave it unscathed. A man would *need* to be dead to survive such close confinement with Elizabeth and remain indifferent.

He did not have energy enough to hit the nightstand again. His anger had all been spent or smothered with fatigue. With an intolerable feeling of futility and no other recourse, he submitted to simply relieving himself as he had been instructed to do. He was asleep and sunk into dreams plagued with shame and longing before anyone returned to the room.

Confined and Unvarying Society

e slept better for having eaten. Indeed, other than occasionally bestirring himself to sip some water, Darcy did little but sleep until the sun was high in the sky the following day. He still felt sore and weak, but less confused each time he awoke. With better clarity of mind, however, came the full dawning of the seriousness of his situation, and though his recovery was naturally uppermost in his mind, other considerations soon began to intrude.

Though they had separate rooms, Elizabeth was presumably known by all at the inn to be nursing him unattended. It mattered not whether it was presumed she was a single woman or somehow entangled with him; either circumstance had the potential to wreak havoc on her reputation. His own, therefore, was in equally grave danger, for the most obvious solution was to sacrifice it and marry her.

His heart quivered staccato-like in his chest at the prospect, and he ignored it, as he had done many times before. To marry so far beneath him—into the Bennet family in particular, with its total want of either consequence or connexions—was impossible. Of this, he had already convinced himself a hundred times over. He cast his gaze about, unreasonably anxious that Elizabeth should somehow deduce his thoughts from the heat in his face. She was not there, and his folly made him cross.

Animated by vexation, he heaved himself a little farther upright and reached for the stack of writing paper sticking out over the edge of the nightstand. The pen rolled off it towards the floor, but he caught it without wrenching his neck quite as painfully as last time. Stretching to dip the pen in the ink proved less bearable, and he resolved the matter by bringing the well down from the nightstand and wedging it against the pillow atop his shoulder.

Thus armed, he began furiously scribbling questions in the hope that the answers might ease his sense of helplessness—or perhaps melt the snow from the damned roads or banish the confounded feelings that flickered unobligingly in his chest at every other moment.

His efforts were to little avail, for even when an entire page of questions lay before him, he was convinced the answers to all of them would still not provide him with the level of information to which he was accustomed. Writing the list all but exhausted him, increasing his concerns for his state of health, as did the unrelenting pain in his throat occasioned by holding his head at the angle required to see what he wrote. Ignorance and weakness were two things Darcy had never tolerated well, and they, along with his growing concern for Elizabeth, began to well and truly sour his mood.

Where she was, he could not suppose. He did not think she was in her room, for the only sounds he had heard since waking were his own hoarse breathing and the odd muffled clatter from below stairs—but even if she were that close, he was powerless to discover it, for he could not call to her. He could not so much as squeak without succumbing to virulent and excruciating spasms. And if she were farther afield, what then? He would barely be able to help her were she sitting at the end of the bed—there was nothing he could do to protect her if she had been foolish enough to venture out of the inn.

His concerns were on the cusp of taking a far darker turn when Elizabeth abruptly appeared at the door from the landing. Fuelled in part by relief and in part by the worst of his fears, he dashed off another hasty question at the top of the page.

"Good day, Mr Darcy," she greeted him, and her tone instantly trebled his concerns. She was very evidently tired and, judging by the paleness of her countenance, possibly distressed. Her attire was ruffled and muddied, proving she *had* ventured out of doors, yet she wore neither bonnet nor gloves. Any stable hand, vagabond, or potboy could have mistaken her for a serving girl and treated her accordingly.

"I see you are feeling much more like yourself today," she remarked, walking across the room to put down something she had been carrying.

"*Are you in good health, madam?*" Darcy demanded, eager to know.

Elizabeth came closer, watching his lips as she approached him. He repeated his question, and, at length, she confirmed that she was tired but not unwell. Glancing at his list, she added, "What have you been writing that has put you in such a fine humour?"

"*Questions,*" he replied, though he did not feel it was an easy word to lip read and pre-empted her bewilderment by simply handing her the top sheet of paper.

The list might have felt inadequate to Darcy, but it did at least have the immediate effect of returning some colour to Elizabeth's cheeks. She dropped her hands to her sides with her fists clenched, blithely crumpling that which had taken nearly all his reserves to compose.

"Where *'the devil'* have I been?" she quoted in an angry tone.

Ruing the hasty addition of such an ill-tempered question, Darcy mouthed an explanation. *"I knew not where you were."*

"No, indeed, for I did not tell you. I am afraid you will not find me as complying as some of your other friends, Mr Darcy. I shall go where I please when I please, and I require neither your permission nor your persuasion to do it."

Puzzling at her meaning, he replied, *"Of course you do not require my permission, but you might have informed me. I was concerned for you. For all I knew—"*

"I cannot understand what you are saying—and neither do I wish to!" she interrupted, before turning on her heel and striding to her bedchamber, slamming the door behind her. Darcy instinctively reached after her, despite how it wrenched his neck. He scarcely managed to lift himself clear of the pillows— only far enough that the inkwell slipped from his shoulder and spilled its contents over his bandages, shirt and bed sheets. He swore—or tried to. Swearing was much less gratifying when no bloody sound came out. Instead, he thumped a fist onto the bed—an equally dissatisfying gesture, for the mattress absorbed what little force he could muster.

With a bitter sneer, he tossed all the writing instruments back onto the nightstand and attempted to regulate his breathing, for the more agitated he grew, the tighter his throat seemed to close. The bandages around his neck felt even more restrictive and suffocating than usual. The spilt ink pulled the skin of his shoulder taut as it dried. He felt filthy. He longed for a hot bath or a change of clothes. To simply get out of bed and walk about the room would be a relief. He rubbed his hands over his face and said a silent prayer begging for release from his ever-worsening misery.

A door clicked open. Darcy lowered his hands but did not move his head, for it hurt too much. When Elizabeth came into view, he was relieved, if surprised, to see that in place of her previous anger, she now looked rather chagrined.

"I apologise, Mr Darcy. I was in an ill humour, but I ought not to have been uncivil."

Darcy held up his finger in rebuttal, then used it to point at himself. *"Nay, I am sorry. It was an ungentlemanly question."*

She squinted at his lips and shook her head. "Where is the pen?" she said, more to herself than to him, for before he could answer, she reached directly over the narrow bed to retrieve it from the nightstand on the other side. She halted directly above him, her arm still outstretched, upon noticing the state of his shirt, whereupon she bit her lips together in an obvious attempt not to laugh, curled her arm back into her side, and eventually straightened again. It was not a moment too soon, for Darcy had been holding his breath since she leant over him and was in dire need of air.

"Oh dear," she said with a small smile. "You will have to buy Lieutenant Carver a new shirt."

He recoiled as her remark sent him spiralling from the heady exhilaration of her form all but laid atop his to the deepest mortification. "*Lieutenant Carver?*"

"He is a guest here," Elizabeth explained. "He was good enough to lend you a fresh shirt when we arrived."

"*This is not then my shirt?*"

"Yours was no longer fit to be worn."

He continued to stare at her, appalled, and she grew visibly more displeased.

"You had no luggage of your own. *I* thought it was very kind of him, but if you th—"

"*You undressed me?*"

Comprehension loosened the knot of vexation marring Elizabeth's brow and widened her eyes in embarrassment. "Oh! No, sir!" she replied with a breathless little laugh. "The gentlemen who carried you up here took care of that while I changed into one of Mrs Stratton's gowns."

A torrent of relief was followed by renewed concern, which he attempted to articulate with the clearly enunciated enquiry, "*Why change gowns?*"

"Mine were all in my trunks somewhere under the snow. Indeed, they still are, for by the next morning when Master John said he would return to fetch them, the snow was too deep to pass."

"*But what happened to the gown you were wearing?*" It was necessary for him to repeat this twice more before she comprehended.

"Oh, I see. Well, as I said, you bled a good deal."

Darcy said a private oath. He had, in the past, allowed himself the occasional luxury of imagining lavishing Elizabeth with the very finest gowns. Now he had ruined the only one in her possession—by bleeding all over it, no less.

"*I shall replace it,*" he promised. He was not convinced she understood what he said, for she did not respond to it directly and continued to look uneasy.

"Mr Darcy, while we are discussing the matter of debts, I must tell you that I had no choice but to use the money you were carrying on your person, for what little I had with me also remains in my uncle's carriage out in the snow. I have kept a tally of everything I have spent, as well as everything we have borrowed or consumed."

"*There is no need.*"

"There is every need!" she replied indignantly. "I shall not allow it to be put about that I am in receipt of gifts or subsistence from any man who is not my relative."

Darcy winced at the indelicacy of the further misunderstanding and mouthed exaggeratedly to eliminate any possibility of misunderstanding, "*I meant only that I trust you.*"

"Oh." She flushed a little and looked at her hands, as she often did when she was uneasy. After an uncomfortable pause, she took a deep breath and continued. "Mr Timmins has been most generous, but we shall have to pay him for the lodgings, food, and candles at least. Oh, and the feed for your horse. Then there was your shirt from Lieutenant Carver, my gown from Mrs Stratton, the paper and ink from Mrs Ormerod, the—"

"*I shall settle it all.*"

"Pardon?"

"*I shall*—" He stopped and mimed writing something instead. "*Any more ink?*"

Elizabeth appeared relieved to have some manner of activity, for she moved with alacrity around the foot of the bed to the nightstand on the other side. There she poured a drop of water from the ewer into the inkwell and swirled it around with the pen.

"We do this at home occasionally. It makes for frightful letters, but it lasts longer. You will despise us for it, no doubt, but there it is."

He did not oblige her by objecting, for he well knew it to be nonsense. On the contrary, he was gratified to have been told as much, as though being privy to such a thing marked a greater intimacy with Elizabeth than others were permitted. He watched her deftly drag the pen around the inside base of the well to ensure no ink went unused and wondered how often she had performed the task. She would never want for ink at Pemberley.

"There." Elizabeth held the paper and newly inked pen towards him. "Now, what were you attempting to say?"

It took him a moment to recall, for his mind had emptied of all else but the vision of Elizabeth at the writing desk in the yellow morning room. At length he wrote,

I shall settle any debts accrued.
And replace your uncle's carriage.

She began to object to this, and he forestalled her by adding,

It is the very least I can do. You have saved my life.

"But your life would not have been endangered were it not for me." She raised an eyebrow and smirked at him. "I have been used to your reasoning being less easily gainsaid, but I shall forgive you this once since you *have* been injured, and on my account." She did not allow the conversation any further latitude and instead held up his crumpled list. "These questions are more sensible. I will answer them as best I can, if you are not too tired?"

Darcy agreed with a smile and watched as she pulled a chair closer to the bed and made herself comfortable in it. Mrs Stratton's dress was too large for her; it masked the lightness of her figure. The excess fabric ruched and slid over her hips in exactly the route a hand might take were it to navigate the same curves.

"Very well, question one."

Darcy started, clenched his jaw to keep from mouthing an oath, and forced himself to attend to the matter at hand.

Elizabeth smoothed the crumpled list upon her thigh with the palm of her hand and read aloud his first question, about the length of his indisposition, then answered, "Today is Friday. The accident occurred on Tuesday. You were insensible for much of Wednesday and Thursday."

Almost three days. That would explain the beard.

"I have answered this next question twice already," she said, and he was poised to beg her forgiveness when she looked up and smiled wickedly at him. "'Tis a good thing I know you to be such an ill-humoured man, else I might think you meant to tease me by asking me to repeat myself so often."

Darcy could not look away from the bewitching glimmer of challenge in her eyes and certainly had not the wits about him to invent an adequate riposte before she grew impatient and continued without one.

"There is the innkeeper, Mr Timmins, and his nephew, Master John. A merchant from Bristol—Mr Stratton, and his wife. Mr and Mrs Ormerod. Mr Ormerod is a parson. Lieutenant Carver—a soldier, obviously—and Mr Latimer, who claims to be an actor, but whom I believe may just be overfond of wine and verse."

Darcy chuckled and instantly regretted it for it made him cough, which was agonising. Elizabeth passed him the glass of water, and though he was grateful, he wished to God he could cease appearing so confoundedly infirm before her. To cover his mortification, he took up the pen and wrote,

Not many people.

"No, but enough, for it is a very small inn—and full."

Fortunate they had rooms for us then.

She smiled faintly and returned to looking at the list. "The next two questions have the same answer, I suppose. Mr Timmins is a dear man, but he has some manner of affliction that affects his posture. His back is stooped, and he seems to suffer weakness on one side of his body. His nephew cannot be older than my youngest sister, for he still has the voice of a choirboy. Mr Ormerod is seventy if he is a day, and his wife is as frail as he is ancient. I have yet to see Mr Latimer sober enough to stand up without listing, and Lieutenant Carver is in possession of only one of his legs. I doubt either of them could outrun a snail. Mr Stratton has no discernible affliction other than being a tradesman, and that does not trouble me half as much as I am sure it troubles you. He is never apart from his wife, and I have no reason to suspect that either of them are not respectable people.

"So you see, I have reasonable cause to believe myself safe, but nobody upon whom I could reasonably impose to help me tend to you, or whom you would be content to do so."

There was something mesmeric about the way Elizabeth presented an argument. She was pert without being impertinent, factual without being prosaic, teasing without being cruel. It made Darcy wish to disagree with her simply to hear more. He picked up the pen.

What about your uncle's coachman?

"He left with Merryweather—Mr Stratton's man." His puzzlement must have been obvious, for she shifted impatiently in her seat and began again. "The coach in which I was travelling overturned, as you know. Mr Stratton was the only person here with another, and he very generously lent us the use of it to transport you back here. His man and my uncle's then returned with the carriage to the scene of the accident to collect—" She faltered. Darcy mouthed the deceased man's name for her, at which she nodded gratefully and continued. "It was their intention to deliver him to London and inform my uncle of what had happened. It can only be assumed that they, too, have been hampered by the weather, for no help has arrived and Merryweather has not returned with the carriage."

She paused to sip some water. Darcy knew not whether they were limited to one glass by circumstance or whether she had unconsciously drunk from his. Either way, it gave him a strange thrill.

"In regard to what I have told people of our situation, the answer is as little as possible," she said, returning to the list. "We are neither of us known in this area, so it matters little what assumptions have been made. I hope we shall be gone soon enough to be quickly forgotten."

He yearned to assure her he would do whatever it took to protect her reputation, but such promises were not in his power to give. He watched her, shamed to consider what she must think of his reticence. She kept her eyes downcast, however, and he could not guess her opinion.

"I confess, I do not know the answer to your question about provisions. Mr Timmins does not appear to be short of supplies, though we are obviously in want of anything fresh."

That was concerning.

Can someone not be sent on foot for more? This Stratton fellow, or the young lad?

Elizabeth, leaning forward to read his scribblings, sat back and began her objections before he finished writing. "Master John insists that if the lower road is blocked, then the high road beyond the rise will be worse. And I know the lower road is blocked, because I tried to get through this morning and could not."

Darcy whipped his head up to look at her so quickly that stabbing pain ricocheted along his neck. He gritted his teeth against it and stared in disbelief at Elizabeth until his pain subsided sufficiently that he could unclench his jaw and mouth furiously, *"That is where you went this morning?"*

Elizabeth's fleeting look of surprise morphed instantly into her more usual defiance. "Aye, sir, it was."

"Alone?"

"Yes. I am aware you think walking alone is terribly unfashionable, but as we have already established, I am scarcely overrun with individuals who might have accompanied me."

Darcy shoved the pen into the inkwell—too hard, for the end of the nib cracked.

To hell with fashion! What if you had come to harm?

He cast her a fierce glance at the end of each sentence for emphasis.

You know neither the way nor the lay of the land beneath the snow.

When so much watery ink had run from the broken nib as covered most of what he had written, he abandoned it and mouthed the words instead. *"Damn it, Elizabeth, what if you had taken a fall?"*

Elizabeth remained still for longer than it usually took her to read his lips. He knew not what emotion held her thus, but her silence made the rasp of his quickened breathing seem stentorian by comparison. With a concerted effort to compose himself, he mouthed in a more controlled manner, *"Why did you attempt it?"*

She looked away and frowned, twisting her mouth curiously as though mulling something over. When she answered, it was said to the far side of the room.

"I wished to post the letters I have written to my father and uncle begging for their assistance. I made it quite far—far enough that my hopes were raised. But I could not even see where the road was, once I got beyond the rise, and by then I was cold and muddy." She gave a sardonic little huff of laughter and returned her gaze to his. "Mud has never troubled me, as I am assured you know, but I detest being cold."

She had written, *begging* for assistance. Her distress settled as a tangible weight upon Darcy's shoulders. For all her courage, she was miles from her family with neither possession nor protection—ostensibly alone, for he was of no use to her. She had witnessed one man die and another get as close to it as be damned, and she wished to go home. And he could not comfort her in any meaningful way.

He turned the ink-stained sheet of paper over and scratched out a plea of his own on the reverse.

I beg you would not attempt it again—if only for my peace of mind. We are strangers here. There is no guarantee you would be safe. Let one of the men deliver your letters.

She finished reading at the same moment he finished writing, and they raised their eyes to each other's in unison. He was vastly relieved when she gave a reluctant nod. He smiled his appreciation and returned pen to paper—though the words danced disconcertingly on the page before his eyes.

I shall write to my cousin when the snow begins to melt. He is in the army. He will send men to clear the ro—

The cracked nib of the pen gave way beneath his leaden grip and scudded across the bed.

"Where is Miss Bingley when she is needed?" Elizabeth said lightly, taking the pen from his hand. "She will kick herself when she learns that you genuinely required her services."

A smile crept across Darcy's lips to lift the heavy corners of his mouth. He well recalled Elizabeth hiding her smile behind her book while Caroline Bingley fluttered around him one evening at Netherfield making overtures about his sister and offering to mend his pen.

"*She is not as awful as you believe,*" he attempted to mouth, though his lips did not form the words well. His throat had begun to throb—a new and worrying development.

"I do not recall ever expressing such an opinion, Mr Darcy."

The mischief in Elizabeth's expression produced a palpable flurry in his gut. "*No need. I know well enough when you despise someone.*"

She watched him say it, and when she had deciphered his meaning, her look of amusement intensified. "Indeed?"

He nodded, too sleepy to remember not to do so, and the pain it incurred was sickening. The room swung around him, and he grabbed at the bedclothes to prevent himself sliding to the floor. When the spinning slowed to a halt, he blinked his eyes open to discover Elizabeth standing over him with an expression of unalloyed compassion. It was a look he had jealously watched her direct at her friends and family back in Hertfordshire, one he had coveted for a very long time.

"You ought to sleep now, Mr Darcy."

"*I am well,*" he insisted mutely. He did not wish to sleep. He wished to talk more to her, to make her smile again, to ease her mind, if he could.

"You are *not* well, sir. You can barely hold a pen. You must rest."

To his surprise, she stepped forward and tugged and smoothed the blanket to better cover him. It was such a comforting gesture it quite disarmed him and without meaning to, he found himself divulging something of his unease. "*I ought to be improving by now.*"

"It has been little more than two-and-seventy hours since you were almost killed. You *ought* to be resting." Elizabeth's eyes moved over him as she checked his covers, his pillows, his bandages. His eyes remained fixed upon her—something she noticed eventually. "What is it?"

"Thank you for helping me."

He could not discern the meaning of the look she gave him. He might have thought it was surprise had not there been something intensely searching about it.

"You are welcome, sir. Sleep now, and I shall heat some more broth for you when you next wake to help rebuild your strength."

Darcy knew not whether it was in the waking world or his dream that she took up his hand and sat beside him until he slept. He did know that if he let go at all, it was long after oblivion claimed him.

A Good Understanding

Unusual noises roused him; clatters, bangs, and the occasional frustrated huff from beyond the door to Elizabeth's bedchamber. He knew not what she was doing, but it sounded as though she was being typically belligerent about it, and that made him smile.

There was another shuffle, another clang, and then the sound of pouring water. An unbidden image of Elizabeth bathing came to mind, and he cursed in vexation, thoroughly ashamed of such ungentlemanly thoughts. By way of distraction, he resolved to attempt to sit up unaided. It worked on both counts, for he managed to both haul himself much farther upright and banish all thoughts from his mind but for the agony of doing so.

He reached for the glass on the nightstand, but water did nothing to relieve his discomfort. Swallowing only radiated pain along his tongue and made the base of his skull thrum. He discarded the glass clumsily on the stand and felt it spill over his hand but could do nothing about it. He held himself still and waited for the pain to ease, though he began to suspect it never would.

While he lay panting in short breaths, Elizabeth emerged from her room. She had not been bathing, but she had apparently washed her hair. She walked bent forwards, with her head tilted to one side as she rubbed it dry with a towel. She started when she saw him and, though Darcy could not be certain in the candlelight, he thought she blushed.

"I thought you were asleep!" Her embarrassment quickly changed to concern upon looking at him properly. "Has something happened? You look very ill."

He could not even bring himself to point at the glass of water in explanation. He wished everything would cease hurting for just a moment.

"You are in pain." It was not a question. She hastened to the side of the bed. "Allow me to rearrange your pillows. They are pushing your head forward, I think." As she had done before, she knelt over him and supported his head as she tugged and batted at the pillows behind him. When she lowered him back down, his pain halved instantly, leaving him wholly at the mercy of the overwhelming surge of yearning for the woman poised above him, with her warm hand at the back of his neck, her wet hair falling all about his face and her breath brushing his forehead.

She retreated a heartbeat later. "Is that better?"

He touched one finger to the back of his other hand. "*Yes.*"

She retrieved her towel and stepped back from the bed, returned to her earlier embarrassment. "Sorry if I dripped on you."

Darcy's mind made yet another unchaste connexion, and he clenched his jaw in annoyance. She deserved far better than to be the object of baser imaginings, yet she had such power over him as frequently rendered him breathless with desire.

The want of any response and perhaps his staring at her wet hair evidently unsettled her. "I could not put up with it another day," she said defensively. He could think of no immediate response, prompting her to continue even more heatedly. "I am aware it is highly improper, sir, but frankly, nothing we have endured these past few days could be considered proper. Compared to blood, gore, and chamber pots, I hardly think my hair being unpinned ought to be what offends you most. I am sure you will survive seeing me in this way!"

Darcy was not sure he would. He signalled for paper and pen, which she grudgingly provided.

Nothing you do offends me.

He showed her, though it only deepened her frown. On a whim, he brought the paper back to his lap and added,

Your hair looks very pretty.

He showed her that also. He did not mistake her blush this time, though he thought she looked more bemused than flattered. She muttered her thanks and left the bedside to sit by the fire.

Ordinarily, Darcy would never have been so ungentlemanly as to watch a lady in any state of undress, but as Elizabeth had so rightly pointed out, there was little either of them could do about their present circumstances. Moreover, she evidently did not object to his seeing, else she would have sat by the fire in her own room. He watched her repeatedly run her fingers the length of her hair until the desire to go to her and perform the task himself became too much to bear, and he forced himself to close his eyes and at least feign sleep, if not actually achieve it.

"Mr Darcy?"

He started, having not heard Elizabeth approach, and carefully rolled his head so as to see her. She was standing at the foot of the bed with her hair loosely rebound and an unusually contrite turn of countenance.

"Forgive me for waking you. I am going downstairs to get some food. I thought you would like to know where I am going."

He smiled warmly at such a conciliatory gesture. She did not leave directly but remained rather awkwardly, unable to meet his eye. Though he knew not what troubled her, he could not but be endeared by her manner, in particular the conscious way in which she rubbed her temple with the tip of her middle finger. Just as he thought he must put her at ease somehow, she found her tongue.

"I beg you would forgive my poor manners, sir. No matter how little I like this situation, I recognise it is not your fault, and that you have even more reason to be unhappy about it than I. It is particularly ungenerous of me to be so captious when you are this ill."

"*Pray, do not concern yourself. I perfectly understand.*"

She smiled lightly. "I have no idea what you just said, but here—" She came forward, holding out the pen. "I mended it for you. It seems only fair that you should have equal opportunity to express your displeasure."

He accepted it, as well as the paper she then passed him, then dipped the pen in the watered-down ink she held out for him.

No apology is necessary.

He held it up and smirked when she rolled her eyes at it, for he was so rarely gainsaid in the normal course of things that it made the challenge of convincing her of his sincerity all the more appealing.

It would be entirely forgivable were you scandalised or inconsolable, yet you have been nothing but attentive. Your courage and dignity amaze me.

He passed her the note and watched her read it. She did not roll her eyes again, though it was not a complete victory for her reply made it clear she still was not persuaded.

"I am beginning to think you *are* teasing me."

"*How so?*"

"One moment you are in high dudgeon, the next you are saying something astonishingly generous. I have not the slightest idea what to expect from you from one moment to the next."

I apologise if I have seemed angry. I am —

He sought for a polite way to explain that unceasing pain and hunger, fear for his recovery, concern for her safety, and the constant battle against his impermissible feelings towards her were somewhat affecting his ability to be civil.

— not feeling myself.

It only made her laugh. "You are more yourself when you are angry than when you are not! It is all this forbearance and generosity that is puzzling me."

He frowned, unsure of her meaning.

"That is more like it," she said with a grin. "I know where I am when you are scowling in that fashion."

Was it her design to vex him into an ill humour simply to prove her point, or was this her real opinion?

You think me an ill-tempered man?

"Mr Darcy, even *you* think you are an ill-tempered man. You told me as much that evening at Netherfield when we were discussing the evils of each other's characters."

He extended a finger in objection, then wrote,

Nay, I said my temper might be considered resentful.

"Oh. And yours is a cheerful sort of resentment is it?" she asked saucily.

He opened his mouth to protest and was exasperated to find that it widened into a smile instead. He could not resist it when she engaged him in this manner. He renewed the ink and his challenge with it.

Perhaps not, but though deep, intricate characters may be no more estimable than those composed of few sentiments, I hope there is more to me than resentment alone.

"Yes, I am beginning to see that," she replied pensively, satisfying him that she had recognised the words as those she had said to him at Netherfield. After a brief pause, she smiled wryly and added, "I meant to apologise, not insult you again. You bring out the worst in me, sir."

The admission set off a minor explosion beneath Darcy's breastbone.

No offence taken, I assure you.

"Then I had better leave before I cause any." She knelt and slid the chamber pot out from under the bed, saying nothing explicit to mortify them both as she held her hands out to help him sit up further—only, "I shall be gone for at least half an hour."

Darcy was inexpressibly grateful for her discretion and for sending up the young boy, John, to remove the spoils before she returned. He was pleased, also, that by then, he had regained some measure of equanimity after the simple task of remaining upright long enough to relieve himself proved so excruciating he could have wept.

Pleasure turned to palpable delight when Elizabeth arrived bearing a fresh serving of broth. He attempted to make less of a spectacle of himself eating this time and managed almost enough to allay his insufferable hunger before discomfort forced him to desist.

"*Have you eaten?*" he mouthed when Elizabeth set aside what was left of his broth.

"Aye, I ate with Mrs Ormerod while I was downstairs. She has promised to give us more of her paper and ink tomorrow."

Darcy smiled. He stopped smiling when she said, "We ought to change your bandages again," for he had not the strength to pretend the notion did not cause him the utmost dismay.

"*Tomorrow.*"

"I know it pains you," Elizabeth said, "But those bandages are covered in ink. And blood." His alarm must have been evident, for she immediately added, "Not a great deal! Only what one might expect from a wound that is not stitched."

It was a stark reminder of quite how far he was from being assured of recovery. There was little he could do but submit; to refuse would have been foolhardy. He did, however, refuse Elizabeth's offer of more brandy, for he had no wish for a repetition of the headache that beset him after his previous indulgence. He would not say the process of peeling away the soiled cloth hurt any more as a result, only that his being more aware gave him far greater cause to be concerned by the pain.

"It looks better," Elizabeth said of his exposed neck once she had cleaned it. "Should you like to see?"

"*No,*" he mouthed without hesitation. "*I would get this over with, if you please.*"

"Of course," Elizabeth said gently, taking up a clean strip of linen. "I shall be as gentle as I can be." She set to work, generously requiring that he need make no attempt to speak. Indeed, they said barely any more for what little remained of the evening, other than his mouthed thanks and her gentle good night as she blew out the candles and retired to her room.

A More Pardonable Pride

I should like to get out of this bed. Would you be so kind as to help me?

So read the note Darcy had ready and waiting for Elizabeth when she emerged from her room the next morning. He had awoken feeling better—not a great deal but improved from the day before—and encouraged by the want of any snow at the window that today might be the day they returned home. He did not show it to her, however, for unlike himself, she seemed to grow more tired with each passing day, and this morning, her red-rimmed eyes bore the unmistakable proof of tears.

He tucked the paper out of sight beneath his pillow and, when she glanced at him, mouthed, *"Is there anything I can do?"*

"Do?" she repeated, coming towards him to better read his lips. "About what, sir?"

"You are upset."

Her surprise was evident, as was her embarrassment. She turned away slightly and rubbed at her eyes with the heel of her palm. Darcy reached to gain her attention with a light touch to her arm.

"I beg your pardon," he mouthed. *"I did not mean to make you uneasy."*

When she made no reply, he reached for the pen and paper, but she forestalled him.

"I understood what you said, Mr Darcy, and it was very considerate of you.

Only, your not *meaning* to embarrass me did not prevent my *being* embarrassed."

He reached for the paper anyway.

> *You would prefer that I not observe your distress?*

Elizabeth gave a wry smile and nodded. He smiled back sympathetically and wrote,

> *I perfectly comprehend. I would infinitely prefer that you not see me in my present state. Permit me to say that of the two of us, you are withstanding the indignity with far more éclat.*

She gave a small, conscious laugh. "I do not know about that. I cannot imagine what pain you must be suffering, yet you do not complain."

> *Neither do you. But you may, if it would help.*
> *Is there a particular matter that has upset you, other than our being detained here?*

He thought twice about whether to expound upon his concerns and, deciding the importance of the matter outweighed the need for discretion, added,

> *Pray, tell me nobody has imposed upon you in any way.*

"Oh, no, nothing of that sort! I was only thinking of my family, and how worried they must be. Jane was already in such low spirits I hardly dare suppose what she must be thinking now."

Darcy remained very still, hoping Elizabeth would go on to talk of her other relatives, whose mention was less incendiary, but she did not. He took it upon himself to mention one of his own instead.

> *I hope my sister does not know I have been waylaid, for it will make her excessively anxious also.*

"How could she not know? Does she not live with you?"
He extended a finger to indicate not.

> *She has her own establishment in Town where she lives with her companion.*
> *We deemed it better that she not be troubled by the comings and goings of an older brother.*

"Troubled by or witness to…" Elizabeth said with a smirk. "A most convenient arrangement for all concerned, I am sure." She did not give him time to object. "May I be so bold as to enquire whom you meant by *we*?"

My cousin and I are joined in the guardianship of my sister.

The ghost of a frown passed over her countenance and, as often occurred with Elizabeth, Darcy found himself revealing more than he intended in an attempt to explain that which was likely of no concern to her at all.

My father hoped that between Fitzwilliam's good humour and my good sense, Georgiana might have some hope of a rounded upbringing.

He could easily discern Elizabeth's delight in this characterisation and basked in her warm smile—until she tipped the matter on its head and he found himself skewered by his own words.

"Even your father thought you were ill-tempered then?"

It was said with a broad grin—an obvious tease—nonetheless, it stung.

He knew me to be serious by nature, certainly. A quality disdained by young ladies in general, I have observed.

She conceded with a chuckle. "I cannot argue with that, as you well know, for you have met my youngest sisters." She pulled up a chair, marking her increased interest in the conversation. "*Your* sister is not silly, though, surely? Can she really give you much trouble?"

Darcy tensed in alarm. Did Elizabeth know of Georgiana's near-ruin? He wished the heightened crackle of his breathing would not so obviously give away his agitation as he wrote,

Have you reason to suppose she might give us any uneasiness?

"None—that was my point. Even *with* one good-humoured guardian, the influences on Miss Darcy must still have been mostly the same as those that influenced you. I wondered if it were not more likely she shared your opinion of pride being a virtue."

Darcy would have sighed with relief had not he thought it might choke him. Far better a conversation about his sister's pride than one of her reputation.

Would that she did.

Elizabeth pulled a face that was a mixture of disapproval and incredulity. "You mean, she is *not* proud, but you wish she were?"

He touched a finger to the back of his other hand—"*Yes!*" When Elizabeth continued to look puzzled, he wrote,

I wish she had learnt to take proper pride in her descent. She loves her family, yet for her, 'Darcy' is but a name. She would throw it away in an instant.

"And what is the name Darcy to you?"
Without hesitation, he answered,

Everything.

Elizabeth read this and turned to him expectantly. "You must have a better explanation than that."

He looked into her eyes. If ever there were a woman clever enough, sensible enough, passionate enough to comprehend the value of all his family had achieved, all it stood for, it was Elizabeth. He had never thought to have the opportunity to discuss it with her and was vastly gratified to observe her evident interest in his answer. It put him in mind to give a fuller reply than he might otherwise have attempted.

The Darcys have always been a just and honourable family. We have opposed many sickening practices and helped advance countless worthy ones. The name represents generations of hard work, ethical investments, liberal thinking, and innovation. Pemberley alone employs hundreds of servants and supports hundreds more tenants and their families.

My sister believes that if she were to give it all up, she would be the only one to sacrifice anything. She has no concept of the very great responsibility we have to all our dependents and to all who have worked hard to make us what we are. For myself, being a Darcy is an honour unequal to any other.

Almost. The *greatest* honour he could wish for was something duty would not permit him to pursue. He jumped slightly when the object of that embargo reached to take the sheet of paper from him.

Elizabeth took her time reading and chewed her lip pensively as she did. The hand in which she held the note was rested on the bed, and close enough that Darcy had only to extend his forefinger to gently brush the back of it to gain her attention. She looked up to meet his gaze over the top of the page, and he raised an eyebrow in query as to her thoughts.

She let out a short sigh. "My good friend Charlotte Collins once said she thought your pride was justified because you had much of which to be proud. I think she may have been right. I mistook you when you defended your pride at Netherfield. I thought you meant to justify your hubris, which is a very different thing and not at all commendable. This"—she indicated what he had written with a glance—"is a very fine sort of pride indeed."

Darcy frowned, and although aware that he was fixing on the wrong part of what she said, could not help but reply, "*Charlotte Collins? Not Lucas?*"

"Oh, yes. She has recently married."

Darcy could hardly keep his countenance. "*Not to your cousin?*"

"Aye, to my cousin—and you may well pull that face. I did try to talk her out of it, for I know he will not make her happy, but she was convinced he—or at least the situation that comes with him—would do for her. She deserved so much better, though! To be partnered with such an obsequious, vain man forever—and knowing that his affection for her was the work of less than four-and-twenty hours and the result of a rejection from another—it was a wretched beginning!"

Feeling a frisson of wariness, Darcy picked up the pen and reached for a new sheet of paper.

By whom had he so recently been rejected?

She winced ruefully when he showed her, though her eyes danced with amusement, and she laughed lightly as she confessed, "Me."

A gulf opened up in Darcy's chest. He felt winded and tried to disguise it by drinking some water, though he suspected anybody with half a mind to look for it would have seen his discomposure.

"It is one of the reasons I decided to travel to London early," Elizabeth went on. "I have not been much in my mother's favour since I refused him. I have felt terribly guilty about it since, for he is the heir to Longbourn, and I have done my family a great disservice in not securing all our futures. Jane would have done it, I am sure. Indeed, I believe Mr Collins could not have chosen a more intractable Bennet sister on whom to pin his hopes, for I think even Lydia would have said yes, if only that it would have meant she was married before the rest of us."

"*Why did you say no?*" Darcy asked, then held his breath.

"Because he is ridiculous, and I have too much respect for myself to submit to such a man."

He let out his breath and almost gagged on the laugh that tried to escape with it, directed fully at himself for the absurd hope that her answer would amount to a confession of longing for him. "*What did your father say?*"

She smiled widely. "That if I married Mr Collins, he would never speak to me again."

Darcy's estimation of Mr Bennet increased tenfold in an instant. His opinion of *Mrs* Bennet remained unchanged, for it was not the first time he had witnessed her attempt to push one of her daughters into a match to which the lady in question was not inclined.

Perhaps your being unaccounted for will better dispose your mother to forgiveness upon your return.

"I should think it will better dispose her to achieve her life's ambition of depleting Hertfordshire's entire supply of smelling salts, but one never knows."

Darcy could not repress his laughter this time, or the horrible wet clack of his closing throat, or the pain that shot up to the roof of his mouth and curdled the contents of his stomach.

"My apologies," Elizabeth said contritely. "It is ungenerous of me to make you laugh—and even more ungenerous to tease my mother. Lord knows she can be a little hysterical on occasion, but she cares a great deal for all of us. She will be very worried about me."

Darcy could have kicked himself for having returned her to worrying about the very thing from which he had been attempting to distract her. Doing his utmost to ignore the renewed pain in his neck, he wrote,

Their concern will be short-lived. It cannot be long before the snow begins to melt and we are able to go home.

He glanced at the window. Elizabeth followed his gaze then stood and crossed the room to look outside. She wrinkled her nose and shrugged inconclusively.

"It has stopped snowing. Any more than that is difficult to tell from up here." She turned to face him. "I shall go down and fetch us something to eat and have a look outside. If it looks as though it has begun to melt, perhaps you could write a letter to your cousin for me to deliver."

Darcy scowled and raised an extended finger in firm objection. *"Not you."*

She tutted and rolled her eyes but conceded. "Very well, for *somebody* to deliver to the village."

Relieved, Darcy held out his arms. *"Would you help me sit up?"*

She complied readily, though when she reached to add another pillow behind him, he pointed at the chair and explained, *"I meant to sit there."*

She pulled back a little to look more squarely at him. "Are you sure? Forgive me for saying, but you still look very ill."

"I am sure."

"As you wish. But one moment." She let go of his arms, pausing in front of him briefly as though she had balanced something breakable in a precarious place and thought it might topple over. When he did not, she stepped away to pull the chair closer.

Somewhere between pushing himself off the bed and lowering himself into the seat, Darcy began to wish profoundly that he had remained where he was. He was every bit as weak as he had expected and lightheaded with the pain of holding his head upright. He was glad at that moment to be mute, for he suspected whatever he might have said were he able to speak would have been distinctly improper.

"There," Elizabeth said when he was in the chair. "Are you comfortable? Oh, foolish question, I can see that you are not—but are you content to sit there while I go downstairs?"

He managed a wan smile, certain the only thing worse than remaining in the chair for any length of time would be the agony of attempting to get out of it again so soon. Elizabeth dithered a little longer but decided in the end to take him at his word and left. Other than resting his head on the high back of the chair, Darcy remained completely still for some time after she had gone, the sound of his rattling breathing filling the room.

Eventually, the prospect of achieving nothing more than to remain conscious until Elizabeth returned vexed him into action. He gingerly stretched his limbs and arched his aching back. With his hands on the armrests, he pulled himself forwards until he was within reach of the water jug on the nightstand. He did not trouble himself to empty it into the basin but brought it to his lap and used his hand to splash cold water directly from it over his face, hair, and hands. He had not the strength to get the thing back onto the stand and instead set it on the floor. With his very last reserves, he gritted his teeth and hauled himself out of the chair.

He could not yell, but a God-awful sound escaped him, almost more alarming than the pain in his neck, that made him think he had ruptured something vital. He staggered the few steps to the bed and half fell, half rolled onto his back and knew nothing after his eyes closed on the brown stain in the centre of the ceiling.

Sound Judgment

"If I am forbidden from walking to the village alone, then *you* are forbidden from getting in or out of that bed again without my assistance. Is that clear?"

Darcy's eyes had not yet opened far enough to blink away the blur of daylight before he received this angry set-down from Elizabeth. It brought him to his senses more quickly than he was used to, though he could not say he did not enjoy the novelty of being scolded. He rolled his head cautiously to look at her and was diverted to see her with hands on hips and cheeks tinged by pique. *"Have you been waiting long to upbraid me?"*

She scowled over his words, mouthing them along with him as she unpicked his meaning. "You frightened me!" she explained angrily once she had. "I came back expecting to find you in that chair, and instead you were sprawled here insensible, making a horrible sound as though you would stop breathing at any moment! As if it were not bad enough the first time you attempted it on your own. What on earth possessed you to try it again?"

Darcy sobered and mouthed an apology. *"Forgive me. I needed to lie down."* Agreeable though it was to be the object of Elizabeth's concern, Darcy did not like that she was distressed and made a concerted effort to breathe more shallowly in the hope the unpleasant rasping would diminish. *"Is the snow melting?"* he enquired to distract her, and because he wished to know.

She made a visible attempt to calm herself. "Only a very little," she replied. "But John has offered to try to take our letters to the village for us anyway. I told him your cousin would bring men to clear the road if only we could get word to him."

Darcy smiled with relief and managed to communicate that he would write to his cousin if she passed the pen and paper.

"In a moment. First you must eat something." She crossed to the other side of the room and returned with a bowl. "This broth has a little more substance to it than the last. It ought to help you regain your strength more rapidly, but *take care* swallowing it."

Darcy could have hugged her. She had brought bread as well, which, after chewing excessively with mouthfuls of water, he was able to swallow without incident. By far the most enjoyable aspect of the meal, however, was that Elizabeth shared it with him. She had, until now, eaten downstairs with the other guests. This time, she sat close by with her own bowl of broth balanced in her lap and conversed with him so easily they could have been dining at a table instead of languishing in a squalid bedchamber with him half-undressed and festering in a bed. And unlike every other table at which they had dined together, he was not stuck at the far end with half the population of Meryton between them, preventing his talking to her. They were each other's sole company—as would be the case every mealtime at Pemberley, were she to live there.

"It could do with more salt," Elizabeth remarked, "but I must say, I have tasted far worse in far grander places."

"*Which places?*" he enquired, wondering if she meant Netherfield, where he had dined on more than one unappetising dish.

"Oh no! I suspect my idea of a grand place is a far cry from yours. I shall not be drawn into naming one only for you to laugh at me for it."

"*I would never laugh at you.*"

She was growing faster at reading his lips and replied almost instantaneously. "Perhaps *laugh* was the wrong word. I can readily believe you would never do *that*. I am of a mind to teach you how, though, for teasing a person is always kinder than despising him."

"*I see little difference—both are forms of contempt.*" Disliking the implication that he would do either, he appealed for pen and paper, which Elizabeth swapped for his empty bowl, freeing his hands to write.

I would not despise anyone, least of all you, for having seen less of the world. Are you sure it is not your own feelings you are imposing on the matter—that actually you are embarrassed by your own unworldliness?

"Yes, quite sure," she answered quickly, though there wavered a look in her eyes as hinted at a greater uncertainty than she professed. "By the same token, I could ask whether you are unjustly proud of your worldliness—whether you think less of anyone who does not possess experiences and knowledge equal to your own?"

I would think less of any person who had no wish to experience or learn about the world. That is not the same as holding them in contempt for not having had the means to see it.

Elizabeth frowned as she read this, though more pensively than quarrelsomely, Darcy thought. Indeed, she betrayed no particular desire to oppose him when she sat back in her chair and enquired whether he had visited many places.

"*Quite a few,*" he replied.

"Which is your favourite?"

"*Pemberley.*" He wondered if he would need to write the name or give an explanation of it, but she appeared to recall it from their conversations at Netherfield.

"It is very quaint that you should prefer your own house to any other place, but that is not quite what I meant. Allow me to rephrase. Which was the most impressive?"

He did not even attempt to mouth the answer and instead committed it to paper where it would be better understood.

Le Château de Versailles.

Elizabeth's eyes widened, and she looked up from the page with an expression of ingenuous wonder that rendered her even more handsome than usual. "Truly? That is enough to make me envious in earnest. Would that you *could* speak, for I should dearly love to hear you describe it."

"I should dearly love to take you there," Darcy thought, though more things than Napoleon's army stood in the way of such a wish.

"All this you have seen, and still your favourite place in all the world is Pemberley?"

"*It is.*"

"It must be quite a house."

"*It is my home,*" he mouthed.

She regarded him intently, and disliking not knowing what she thought, he took up the pen and wrote,

Have you been to many places? You cannot have always been at Longbourn.

She did not reply directly upon reading this. First, she tore off a small piece of bread roll and ate it, all the while peering at him dubiously. "I am not sure I wish to know why that is your opinion," she said presently. "I am certain it is your design to be severe on *somebody.*"

He regretted making such an inelegant compliment, for he ought to have known Elizabeth would see directly past it to his slight upon her family.

"But you are right," she continued. "My mother's father had a house in

Hampshire, and I visited him there often before he passed away. He was a dear, gentle man—calmer and, dare I say, more sensible than his wife or daughters. Much like his son, my Uncle Gardiner, with whom Jane and I spent a good deal of our childhoods. He and his wife have a house in London. I am due to travel with them this summer, as it happens. To the Lakes. I have never been before. I am excessively impatient to see it."

Darcy felt an irrational resentment for these relations with the privilege of seeing Elizabeth's face as she beheld that sight for the first time. Like as not they knew none of the best places to show her, or any of the finest establishments in which to stay. He briefly wondered whether, if he could discover when they meant to go, he might engineer a chance encounter—until he recalled that his present predicament was the result of a similar scheme and chided himself for his foolishness.

"If you object so violently to my connexions, I wonder that you troubled yourself to enquire about them," Elizabeth said tersely, dropping what was left of her roll into her empty bowl.

"*Pardon?*"

"You cannot deny your disdain, sir. You frowned at the mere mention of my visiting my uncle in Cheapside."

I was not frowning, and you made no mention of their living in Cheapside—only London.

Darcy surprised himself with the latter, for it was less than completely honest. Though Elizabeth had not mentioned it, he knew full well her relations lived in that part of Town, for the information had been passed on with great relish by Miss Bingley when they were at Netherfield.

Still, it gave Elizabeth pause. She opened her mouth to object, closed it again, nodded to herself, and said instead, "Very well. But, pray tell me—in *truth*—now that you know they live in the City, will you still credit them with having had such a favourable influence on me?"

If they are the relations from whom you learnt your sense and disposition, then I credit them with a great deal.

"And their condition in life does not diminish your opinion of them?"

The ink ran from the pen to blot the page where Darcy pressed it as he thought overlong on how to answer. The situation of Elizabeth's relations was one of the paramount objections to his marrying her. It would be a falsehood to claim otherwise. Yet, he could have no objection to the individuals, having never met them, and, judging by this conversation, possibly ought even to admire them. This, he supposed, was Elizabeth's meaning.

A sudden flush assailed him as he wondered at her deeper purpose. He felt compelled to remind her that even were her relations the best people in the world, they would never be *his* relations.

The condition in life of anyone so wholly unconnected to me is immaterial.

After reading this, Elizabeth fixed her eyes on him and tipped her head sideways, as a hawk does when judging the distance to its prey. "The sense and worth of anybody outside of your circle is not important then?"

"Not particularly," he thought, surprising himself again. Rattled and a little ashamed, he deflected the conversation back to her by writing,

You take great delight in questioning my judgment. Are you confident your own is always sound?

The parade of expressions that crossed Elizabeth's countenance suggested it was not a matter she had ever before considered. He was unsurprised that the sentiment upon which she settled last was amusement.

"As certain as anyone ever is, I suppose. I take your point."

He almost pressed the matter, for it seemed the perfect opportunity to query something that had been troubling him since the day before, but he decided against it. Quite apart from the possibility of his not liking her answer, there were weightier concerns to attend to. He thanked her for the broth and the conversation but suggested they set both aside that he might write a letter to his cousin.

The Influence of Friendship

"It really is a good thing that Miss Bingley cannot see you at present. Though I am sure she would forgive you a great deal, I wonder if even she could overlook the unevenness of those lines."

Darcy attempted to glare at Elizabeth but could not long suppress a smile. It was true; dashing off a few lines of conversation had been relatively easy even in his recumbent position, but composing a legible letter was proving impossible. The pain in his neck prevented him holding his head forward to see the page properly and squinting at it aslant meant his letters sloped pitifully across the page.

"Should you like me to write it for you?" Elizabeth asked more sympathetically, to which Darcy acceded by handing her the pen and paper. She declared what he had written to be illegible and began afresh, transcribing the salutation from the original. "Does this say *Fitzwilliam*?"

Darcy absentmindedly touched the back of one hand with the finger of another, distracted by how Elizabeth's lips formed around the word.

She wrote it down. "I cannot read the rest so I shall improvise." The glint in her eye and slight curl of her lip gave Darcy to hope some manner of devilry was imminent. His stomach turned over in anticipation.

"Colonel Fitzwilliam," she began. "Pray, send help—no, help will never do. *Reinforcements* is better. Send reinforcements. I have been hurt—no, *incapacitated*. I am stuck—I am *imprisoned* at an inn near Spencer's Cross. The road is blocked—" She tapped the end of the pen against her front teeth while she thought. "The road has been *barricaded* by snow. I require…*evacuation*."

"*What are you about?*" Darcy mouthed when she glanced at him slyly.

She fixed him with a look of such impishness as made his heart thump. "Studying for words of four syllables." He narrowed his eyes at her, and she let slip a small laugh. "I am merely attempting to make it sound authentic. You would not like your cousin to dismiss the letter as a hoax."

He held out his hand to take the pen and stack of paper from her and wrote, albeit messily, on a different page,

> *Bingley was wrong to imply that my use of long words is affected. It scarcely ought to reflect poorly on me that my vocabulary is more comprehensive than his.*

Elizabeth's smile faded. "Forgive me, Mr Darcy. I was only teasing, but I forget that you do not care for being laughed at."

Yet more rattled than before, he handed back the writing apparatus, keeping his eyes downcast. "*It was Bingley's teasing I disliked,*" he mouthed sullenly. "*I enjoyed yours.*"

It seemed a long while before he heard the scratch of the pen resume.

"It was most uncivil of Mr Bingley to tease you at Netherfield when he must have known you would not like it," Elizabeth said. "Perhaps he is not quite as deferential towards you as he claimed to be."

Unable to guess whether she meant to defend him against Bingley's teasing or defend Bingley against *his* supposed tyranny, Darcy made no reply.

"There," Elizabeth declared. "I am finished. Will that do, do you think?"

He read what she showed him and assured her it would do very well.

"Here then," she said, holding the pen out to him. "You had better sign it."

He did, and she blew on it to dry the ink. "F. Darcy," she read with interest. "Would it be terribly impertinent to enquire what the F stands for?"

"*Fitzwilliam,*" he mouthed.

"Fitzwilliam?" she repeated with a frown, as though she had misread his lips. "The same as your cousin's surname?"

"*In honour of my mother,*" he replied with a small shrug that nonetheless sent pain lancing down his neck. Elizabeth pulled a face that he hoped was approval, though he had given up attempting to know her thoughts and resolved not to count on it. Instead, he determined to settle another matter that troubled him still and indicated that he wished her to hand back the stack of paper. In a mortifyingly childish scrawl, he wrote,

> *What was your meaning when you said that you were not as complying as my other friends?*

She smiled ruefully upon reading it. "I ought not to have said that, sir. It was uncivil, and I apologise."

> *Nevertheless, I would know your meaning.*

"Very well," she said, tilting her chin defiantly. "I meant that you appear to like having your own way very well, but that I am not as willing as some of your friends to be at your disposal."

He refrained from gaping at her and mouthed, *"Which friends?"*

"Since we have only one mutual acquaintance, you must know I mean Mr Bingley."

"In what way is he at my disposal?"

"Can you deny you had a part in his leaving Hertfordshire after his ball and not returning?"

Darcy tensed, and it hurt his throat. He ought to have stuck with his first instinct and not enquired. *"Bingley had business in—"* He gave in and took up the pen instead.

> *Bingley had business in London. Why do you suppose I had anything to do with his decision to leave?*

"It is speculation, I confess," Elizabeth answered. "Based on the opinion you once expressed to me that, where there exists a satisfactory degree of intimacy between friends, and where the matter is of enough importance, one party might justly argue the other into complying with their wishes."

> *And what makes you believe—*

The pen ran dry. He dipped it in the ink Elizabeth held out and finished.

> *—it was my wish that Bingley not return to Hertfordshire?*

"A few things," she replied with a display of equanimity incongruous to the turn of the conversation. "But mostly the letter Miss Bingley sent to Jane shortly afterwards with the information that her brother was in Town courting your sister. Indeed, she dwelt with some warmth on how much the relations of both parties wished the connexion."

Darcy froze, dismayed to feel himself redden.

"I knew you were aware of Mr Bingley's partiality towards Jane, for I was there when Sir William mentioned it to you. And when my mother so"—she rolled her eyes—"*discreetly* boasted of their attachment within your hearing. Given all of that, perhaps you can forgive me for concluding that you would prefer your friend to stay away from my sister and increase his intimacy with yours instead. But if I have misread the situation, then I apologise."

She was too clever for her own good. Nay, he corrected himself, too clever for *his* good. There was no evading the matter now; he would not lie to her.

> *You have not entirely misread it.*

He paused to sip some water and collect his thoughts. Doing his utmost not to be perturbed by the manner in which she watched him, he adjusted himself slightly on the bed and resumed writing as well as he could, which was not very.

> *I advised him to avoid raising your sister's (and the neighbourhood's) hopes any further, but my object was not to secure his affections for my sister.*

His unwieldy scribblings meant he ran out of ink rapidly. He dipped the pen again.

> *I shall not deny such a match would be desirable, should it come to pass, but Georgiana is too young at present to entertain any suitor.*

"What then *was* your object in separating him from Jane?"

"*Not a good match,*" he mouthed, too tired to lift his arm to dip the pen in the ink again. "*Would have made him unhappy.*"

He could tell it vexed her. Indeed, he had not for a moment thought it would not, but the intensity of her displeasure startled him. Surely, with her good sense, she could comprehend the imprudence of the union.

"Why was it for you to decide what would make Mr Bingley happy?" she demanded. "Or my sister? Or yours, for that matter, for Miss Darcy might very well prefer not to marry a man who loves somebody else now— but I suppose that consideration was of no consequence to you when you were arranging it all to your liking." She banged the inkwell down on the nightstand, evidently too cross to oblige him by holding it any more. "Do you see no injustice in the fact that *you* are marrying where you like, yet you refuse to allow anybody else in your sphere of influence the same privilege?"

She gave no indication of having heard his heart's thundering misstep, though it did so loudly enough that Darcy would not have been surprised if she had. He had been so careful to give her no indication of his regard! How had she come to think they could ever marry?

"*What?*" he mouthed feebly, unable to express aught more eloquent.

"Do not pretend ignorance, sir. You do not play the part well. I know you are marrying your cousin."

He did gape at her then, and though he would never have thought incredulity could actually hurt, fire coursed down his neck. "*I am not marrying my cousin,*" he mouthed, unsure whether he was more relieved or disappointed that she had not mistaken his intentions after all.

She slumped a little in her chair with a chagrined expression, though it soon transformed into churlishness. "Why not? What is wrong with *her*?"

"*Nothing! I simply do not wish to marry her.*"

Elizabeth shook her head disbelievingly. "You have done a much better job of showing your hypocrisy with this than I could ever hope to. You will not marry your cousin because you do not wish to, yet you perceive no value in the wishes of the people whose lives you arrange so high-handedly?"

Darcy had not the fortitude for this! He was not used to accounting for himself and certainly not whilst unable to speak. "*I have forced nobody to do anything against—*" He ceased his silent defence, for Elizabeth was squinting at his mouth and shaking her head in exasperation. He indicated that if she wished him to respond, he would require more ink, and she very reluctantly placed the well back within his reach. It was running dry, and it was necessary for him to dip the pen thrice more before his reply was done, by which point his arm shook with fatigue.

> *Have forced nobody to do anything against their will. Have only given counsel. My prerogative where my sister & friend are concerned. Only natural I should desire a good husband for the former & I deemed it unwise that the latter sacrifice so much for a lady who would only have accepted him because her mother expected it of her.*

Elizabeth had returned to leaning over him to read as he wrote, thus, when she read this, her twisting to stare at him put their faces in exceedingly close neighbourhood. Either the proximity did not trouble her, or she did not notice in her pique. "My mother may have rejoiced at the match—and she may well have done so in too public a manner for your liking—but I assure you, she would *not* have insisted that Jane accept an offer if it were not her desire to do so!"

He looked into her eyes. "*She expected it of you.*"

Elizabeth recoiled, her countenance clearly showing the perturbation of her mind. She began several angry retorts only to swallow them before they were said. Darcy dipped the pen again, the nib clattering against the side as his hand wavered.

> *Bingley has spent all his adult life striving to raise his family's respectability in the eyes of the world. An often unkind world, I must add. After such endeavours, it would be painful to see him ridiculed for the sake of an unhappy connexion.*

"You believe people would ridicule him for marrying *Jane?*"

Darcy extended his finger. "*Not Miss Bennet, no. But some of your family—*" With barely any ink left in the pen and scarcely the strength to tilt his head far enough to even see the page, Darcy was nonetheless determined to forestall Elizabeth's ire, and he laboriously scrawled,

> *I am sorry to pain you, but you are an intelligent woman; you must see that the behaviour betrayed by your mother, your three younger sisters, & occasionally even your father is not what is expected in the fashionable world. I*

saw you be embarrassed by them often enough to be confident you understand as much.

It was a credit to Elizabeth that despite her evident indignation, she still gave consideration to what he wrote and responded in a measured, if unhappy, tone.

"My family might embarrass me from time to time, but no more than it clearly embarrassed Mr Bingley when his sisters were hateful to their house-guests, or when his brother was a glutton at dinner, or when his *friend* refused to speak to anyone in the neighbourhood because he was too proud to over-look their follies."

Bingley was not embarrassed by me! thought Darcy indignantly. His own circumstances and consequence were superior in every way to his friend's. If anyone had a right to be embarrassed by the connexion, it was he!

Elizabeth said nothing, and in her silence, the old browned walls of the bedchamber pressed inwards, it seemed, making known their silent disdain. Darcy felt altogether less assured. The pretensions of polished society had no relevance here. In this place, he was but a man, with no voice and one foot on the other side of death's door—no better and quite possibly a good deal worse than any of his friends. The unpalatable verdict provoked him to retaliate, for was Elizabeth not just as fastidious?

Did you overlook Mr Collins's follies when you attempted to persuade your friend not to marry him?

"I did—that is, I did not, but..." She seemed genuinely anguished by the objection but still shook her head in contradiction. "It is not the same! Mr Collins did not love Charlotte—and Charlotte most certainly did not love him!"

You would have me believe your sister loved Bingley? I find that difficult to countenance consi—

The ink ran dry and no amount of dipping or scraping the pen in the well could gather enough to finish what Darcy wished to write. Elizabeth shoved her chair backwards to leave and he reached for her hand, desperate that she not go before he could explain. He almost gagged on the pain the forward lunge induced, though his pitiable wheezing did have the advantage of post-poning Elizabeth's departure.

"*I observed them,*" he mouthed, gesturing to his eyes then the imaginary couple. "*She never seemed truly pleased. Never laughed, as you do when you are happy. She only smiled the same way she smiled at everyone.*" To demonstrate his point for Elizabeth, who was peering furiously at his mouth as though searching for words by which to be offended, Darcy affected a smile as benign as any he had seen Jane Bennet bestow upon Bingley. It was indelicate, but—for want of another means of communication—all he had.

"You would condemn her because she was not animated *enough?*" Elizabeth cried. "When you have just vilified the rest of my family for being too demonstrative?"

"Not unanimated — indifferent!"

"And you would know her better than I or Mr Bingley, of course," she replied coldly. "You, who never troubled yourself to speak more than two words to Jane, are ready to declare her heart untouchable because she did not laugh often enough? Perhaps you think my sister Kitty loves Mr Bingley better because she sniggered once in his parlour?"

He pulled an incredulous face.

"Very well, that was facetious, but you take my point? You have convinced yourself there was no affection between them simply because it better suited your wishes to have him marry your sister."

Darcy suddenly felt overwhelmingly tired. Bingley had repeatedly asserted his belief that Miss Bennet returned his affection with sincere, if not with equal, regard. Wherefore, and with what authority, had Darcy presumed to know better? He let out a slow, careful breath, disliking the heaviness in his heart. "Yes," he mouthed, *"I probably have. And I beg you would forgive me."*

He knew not what Elizabeth had been expecting, but it was evidently not an apology. No sooner had she finished frowning at his lips to fathom what he said than she sat back in her seat and blinked at him several times without saying a word herself. She then spent some minutes plucking at the fraying fabric on the arms of the chair, from which she did not look up when she eventually began speaking.

"Charlotte warned me once that Jane was too guarded in her feelings towards Mr Bingley. Before she married Mr Collins, I used to think Charlotte was the most sensible person of my acquaintance. If *she* believed Jane appeared indifferent, then I...well, I suppose I can understand how you might have thought the same."

It was a gracious concession. He waited for her to look up then mouthed, *"You admire your sister very much."*

"I do," she replied with a wistful smile. "She is the very best of our family —with a composure of temper and uniform cheerfulness of manner that I have *never* been able to emulate."

Darcy smiled, though he did not agree that it necessarily made Jane Bennet the best of them.

"Oh heavens!" Elizabeth said abruptly, then burst out laughing. In answer to Darcy's gesture of enquiry, she pointed at the window. "We really ought to learn to disagree less often. We have been arguing so long it has begun snowing again. Our letters will have to wait."

Irrepressible Feelings

T hough Darcy preferred to think of it as more exposition than argument, their conversation still exhausted him, and he slept until after dusk. Every bit of rest brought a slight improvement, and he awoke to less pain than he had known for several days. It allowed him to better tolerate Elizabeth's ministrations as she redressed his wound once again. His neck, though still throbbing by the end, did so with less alarming intensity, and his breathing seemed to have settled into a steady, dry rattle.

"How does it feel?" Elizabeth enquired. "Does it hurt any less?"

He held up a hand, his thumb and forefinger an inch apart to indicate the mild improvement, then mouthed, *"How does it look?"*

"Not much changed from yesterday. Is your head better? The lump has gone down."

Darcy made the sign for yes; that injury at least seemed to be healing well. *"Is there any warm water left?"* he enquired, desirous of talking about something other than his manifold ailments. He mimed washing his face and felt a fool doing so. He ought not to have, for Elizabeth's smile was all sympathy as she assured him there was plenty.

"Let me find you a clean cloth."

Darcy forestalled her departure with an upheld finger, with which he then indicated the nearby chair. Elizabeth looked in the direction he pointed then back at him, a divertingly sceptical expression on her face. "Truly? After this morning's disastrous attempt?"

"I shall atrophy if I do not regain my feet soon."

She shook her head and laughed lightly. "I am not sure what you just said, but I cannot refuse when you look so wretched. I pity the woman you do eventually marry, for I am quite sure that look will rescue you from all manner of trouble with her."

Darcy was vastly relieved that she walked away as she said this, for he would not like her to see the effect her words had on him. Nonetheless, as he reached for and gulped from his glass of water, almost making himself choke in his haste, he could not expel from his head the notion that this was singularly useful information of which to be in possession.

Elizabeth returned with a washcloth and another garment. "Here is a clean shirt for you, too. This one is Mr Ormerod's. I am not sure it will fit as well, but it is, at least, less inky."

He thanked her sincerely and accepted her help sitting upright and manoeuvring himself into the chair. He gripped the armrests forcefully and fixed his eyes on the floor, willing the pain to ebb. The sound of furniture being scraped across the floor bade him look up. Elizabeth was engaged in tugging the round eating table towards him from the fireside. When it was near enough for him to use, she walked around to the other side and gave it another shove forward until it butted up against both arms of his chair, entrapping him in his seat. He opened his hands wide, palms up, and raised one eyebrow in query.

She grinned a beautifully devilish grin. "This way, if you swoon—which you look in a fair way to do—you will only fall as far as the tabletop. I stand a far better chance of picking you up from there than the floor." She walked behind him to retrieve the washbowl and ewer from the nightstand, both of which she arranged in front of him. Then she retrieved the table mirror from the floor next to the bed and a candle from the nightstand and placed those in front of him also.

Darcy reviled the sight of himself: drawn, dirty, and unshaven. Whilst he did not consider himself a vain man, neither was he unaware of the advantages nature had provided him, and he was dismayed to discover that, in contrast to his usual careful presentation to the world, he now resembled nothing better than a bedraggled vagrant. Appearing thus in Elizabeth's presence afforded a singular kind of mortification. He ran his hand over his fully grown beard, and his reflected self sneered back at him in distaste.

"If there is nothing else, I shall leave you now," Elizabeth said quietly. "Only for ten minutes this time, though. Just in case."

WHEN SHE RETURNED WITH MORE FOOD, DARCY WAS WASHED, CHANGED, AND somewhat miraculously still vertical in his seat. Elizabeth would never know how close pulling shirts on and off over his head had brought him to fulfilling her prediction of falling insensate onto the table.

They ate together again, though this time with less conversation. Whilst Elizabeth appeared content to say no more on the matter, their earlier debate had left a pall over them that Darcy knew not how to alleviate. He could not be certain whether she were angry, distressed, or merely fatigued, yet talkative she was not.

For his part, there was a grave sense of unease. Elizabeth challenged him as no other person ever had, and he disliked enough of what her interrogations revealed of him to be troubled. He held no ill will towards her for doing so. Indeed, he supposed he ought to be grateful that if there really was so much objectionable about his behaviour, she was willing to object to it, for it seemed nobody else would. *Though it is probable,* he admitted to himself privately, *that I would not be as receptive to such critique from any other person.*

"What is it?" Elizabeth said impatiently.

Darcy started, mouthing *"Nothing"* in bemusement.

"Then why are you staring at me in that manner?"

He reached for the pen that had lain on the table next to him throughout their meal and dipped it in the newly replenished ink.

There is nobody else at whom to look.

He held it up for her to see, unable to keep his mouth quite straight, for though it was a most convenient excuse, it was so far from the truth as to be absurd. Were there a hundred people in the room, he would still only wish to look at one.

"Oh," she said, leaning back into her chair after she had read it. Was that disappointment in her tone? "Well, you ought to know that when you look at things, you appear excessively grave."

Darcy was not naturally given to cheerfulness, but in any case, his reflections when he regarded Elizabeth were often so consuming that he did not wonder at his appearance of gravity. It was one of the things that had alarmed him most upon first making her acquaintance, for never had he been so bewitched by any woman as he was by her.

Some things require excessive reflection.

This she read, then, with a small huff, she pushed her bowl away and picked up the book she had been lent by one of the other guests. After staring at the same spot on the same page for a minute or more, she said quietly, "I find it intimidating."

Even had it not been evident in the tone of her voice and turn of her countenance how little she liked making the admission, Darcy would have known. Independence as fierce as hers was bound to chafe against being afraid of anything. After a moment's consideration, he picked up the pen again.

Does it help to know that I find you equally intimidating?

He twisted the sheet of paper to face her and pushed it across the table. She picked it up, and he did not miss the small flash of surprise upon her countenance. After a moment, she gave in to a small smile. "Yes, a little. Though I cannot imagine why you should."

Scarcely about to commit the explanation to paper, Darcy pointed instead at her book, then at himself, then cupped his ear and raised an eyebrow in question.

"You wish me to read to you?"

He smiled hopefully, and to his delight, she consented.

It was so very easy, in the cocoon of the small, remote inn, away from the complications of honour and duty, to lose himself in her voice. Here, he need not torture himself with reminders of why he may not enjoy her company, for they were marooned here and he had no choice. It could wait until they were rescued before he must return to pretending he did not delight in her enjoyment of reading, or the way her larynx danced up and down in her throat when she did so aloud, or the way she brushed her hair from her forehead every time she turned a page.

She reached a diverting passage and giggled slightly as she read it, and something contracted in Darcy's chest. He closed his eyes and allowed himself, ever so briefly, to imagine they were at Pemberley. The image his mind conjured, and the warmth of Elizabeth's tone, afforded him a greater sense of calm than he had felt since the accident. Surrendering to it was the most gratifying thing in the world—until pain ripped him from his dreams.

In confusion and panic, he opened his eyes wide in time to see Elizabeth throw her book aside and dash around the table towards him. He still had not regained his senses sufficiently to comprehend what was happening before she pushed the table away and edged between it and him to take his head in both her hands and tilt it up, holding him face to face with her, their lips mere inches apart.

"I think you must have fallen asleep," she said gently. "Your head fell forwards."

Darcy was transfixed—too surprised to do ought but stare into her eyes, and too overcome with pain to lie convincingly to himself any longer. Returned to laborious, rasping breaths and lightheaded for want of air, he lifted a hand to cover one of hers and squeezed it with something far more significant than gratitude.

"'Tis well," she whispered. "Come, allow me to help you back to bed. You need to sleep."

A Lively Disposition

Darcy awoke the next morning to an empty and strangely hushed chamber. The muffled noises of the inn drifted up from downstairs, but his own surroundings were mired in quiescence. It took him a moment to fathom what marked the change. It was the want of his own clamorous breathing. The constant throb of pain was there still, but so was air, flowing into and out of his lungs without hindrance.

With great caution, he inhaled more deeply than he had dared to in almost a week. His chest filled, his windpipe made only the vaguest objection, and he was flooded with relief such as emboldened him to call for Elizabeth to inform her of the improvement. His voice did not answer the summons. His throat closed around the first syllable, and all the advancement of a moment before was lost as he was returned to the agonising spasms of the previous days.

He sat up instinctively and was almost felled by pain as the movement pulled the edges of his wound taut. He put a hand to his throat and fought against rising panic. He had been breathing with ease a moment ago; he ought to be able to do so again.

The door to Elizabeth's bedchamber opened. She exclaimed upon seeing him and hastened to his side. Darcy raised a hand to assure her he was well, though the rasp of his breathing did little to substantiate the claim, and she apparently mistook the gesture, taking his hand in hers instead and sitting on the edge of the bed with it clasped in her lap.

"Try to calm yourself, sir. It will pass sooner that way. Look at me"—as if he were not already—"and let us breathe in time." Her chest rose and fell as she took slow, exaggerated breaths.

Darcy pulled his hand from hers, turned, and fumbled with the water ewer. Elizabeth had many talents, but slowing his breathing was not among them.

"Allow me." She reached across him to pour some water, his airways filled with the scent of whatever she had used to wash her hair, their fingers brushed as he took the glass from her—none of which was even remotely calming. He took a sip, then another and another before letting out a long sigh and allowing his shoulders to relax.

"What happened?" Elizabeth enquired.

With a wry grimace, he lifted his hand next to his mouth and made a gesture akin to a bird's beak opening and closing.

"You spoke?"

He made an unequivocal cutting gesture with both hands to indicate his total failure to do anything of the sort.

"You are still unable to?"

Her crestfallen expression stirred an unexpected swell of self-pity in Darcy for which he did not care at all. *"Excuse me,"* he mouthed as he tugged the bedclothes aside, unduly angry, yet sick of Elizabeth being witness to his unabating infirmity. She stood from the bed but, to his consternation, rather than moving out of his way, held out both hands to help him to his feet. Her solicitude had quite the opposite effect to that which he knew she intended, for it made him feel such an invalid that he snarled in disgust—a discourtesy he regretted deeply when her countenance showed first surprise and then hardened into something altogether less forgiving.

"Pardon me, Mr Darcy. I was not aware you were recovered enough to stand unassisted." She stepped back and indicated his clear path from the bed with a sweeping wave of her arm.

Darcy was caught by the steely flash in her eyes. He had never known a woman who suited angry sarcasm so well, and he wondered whether she were aware of the endearing little crease that formed at the bridge of her nose when she scowled.

Her expression grew stormier still. "You are diverted now? Truly, you are the most contrary man I have ever known!"

Ordinarily, Darcy would have ceased smiling immediately, for he was not used to his expression being under such poor regulation, but he found he did not wish it. Instead, he smiled more broadly and mouthed a rather insincere, *"Pardon me."*

Elizabeth looked intently at his lips but did not seem to comprehend.

"Sorry," he attempted instead, thinking it might be easier to lip read, but she continued to study his mouth, her expression indecipherable. He could not immediately think of an alternative means of apology so said nothing more, but she did not look away, and therefore neither could he. He noticed, therefore, the small frown flickering about her eyes. He saw when her lips parted

ever so slightly as though she had forgotten what she meant to say. He beheld the very slight shift in colour as her eyes darkened. The longer she stared at him, the faster his heart raced.

Elizabeth took a sudden intake of breath. "You must be desirous of some privacy. Pray, excuse me."

Darcy watched her go—and after the door closed behind her, he watched that for a long while also, his heart now hammering violently. All his struggles to conquer his feelings had been for naught; he knew in that moment his fate was sealed. Duty be damned! It was inconceivable that he not have her by his side to look at him in that manner every day. Breathing erratically and grinning like a fool, he dragged himself, lightheaded but euphoric, into the nearest chair to await her return.

W HEN SHE BUSTLED BACK INTO THE ROOM SOME TIME LATER, IT WAS CLEAR SHE HAD been out of doors. Her skirts were wet, and her cheeks flushed prettily with cold.

"*Is the snow melting then?*"

"Pardon?" she replied distractedly. It was no surprise she had not comprehended him, for she looked away before he finished mouthing the words. He leant gingerly across the table for some paper, reaching it with his fingertips and sliding it towards him to write,

Has the snow begun to melt?

She glanced at the note sidelong. "Oh—no, not at all, I am sorry to say."

Darcy hoped this discovery was not borne of another attempt to walk the unknown route to the village.

Yet you walked out anyway?

She had busied herself emptying her arms of the things she had brought up from downstairs, and Darcy was forced to hold the note out towards her before she would read it. She looked at him sharply afterwards, but then her countenance relaxed into a wry grin. "I wished for some air and exercise." She shrugged. "I got the air—just not the exercise."

"*I envy you even that.*"

"I imagine you are sick of these four walls. Are you warm enough for me to open a window?" Without waiting for him to answer, she walked to do just that.

Delighted at the prospect of some fresh air, Darcy planted his hands on the arms of the chair and steeled himself to stand up.

"What are you doing?" Elizabeth cried.

"*Coming to the window,*" he mouthed, taken aback by her urgent tone.

"For heaven's sake, you have barely regained the strength to sit in a chair. You cannot possibly mean to walk over here unaided and *stand* by the window. You can breathe the air just as well from where you are."

He could not help but laugh, no matter that it made no sound and caused him to cough painfully.

"And what, pray tell, amuses you so about that?" she enquired.

Still wheezing, Darcy sank back into the chair and wrote his reply.

You look just like your sister when you are vexed.

Elizabeth returned to his side and leant over him slightly to read it. "Jane?"

He looked up at her, delighting in her closeness and finally feeling at liberty to enjoy it. "*Miss Lydia.*"

She regarded him strangely, her mouth almost smiling but for the frown of puzzlement that pulled at her brow. "You have a singular talent for insulting people without seeming to, Mr Darcy. I cannot decide whether it is by design or by accident that you continually give offence."

Surprised and a little offended, he hastily returned pen to paper.

You cannot really think I meant to insult you?

"After your recent appraisal of Lydia's behaviour, *you* cannot expect me to believe you drew the comparison in order to compliment me."

She was right: he had been amused precisely because she had appeared less restrained than usual. Whereas her sister's ungoverned behaviour was highly objectionable, the thought of Elizabeth being a little wild pleased him very well indeed. But then, a man rarely desires the same conduct in a sister as he does in his wife. He held her gaze, smiled slightly, and mouthed, "*But I did.*" When she scoffed, he wrote,

High spirits become you.

She turned a familiar expression on him, the glint in her eye promising some mischief or other. "You once told me your feelings were not puffed about with every attempt to move them, but it seems to me they change depending on whatever suits you best at the time. You have now censured my mother and younger sisters for their high spirits, derided Jane for her want of them, and complimented me for mine. I am beginning to wonder if you are half as resolute as you wish everyone to believe." She leant slightly towards him. "*I* think you rather enjoy liveliness but are too afraid to admit it."

He enjoyed hers. A good deal.

In the right place, at the right time, liveliness can be very agreeable.

"Exactly as I thought!" she exclaimed after reading this. "I have found you out, Mr Darcy. In spite of the pains you take to disguise yourself, you are really sick of civility and deference and long for a little of the fun you see the rest of the world having." She grinned widely. "'Tis well. I shall tell nobody. Especially not Miss Bingley, for she would only try to please you by being *un*civil, and she is difficult enough to tolerate when she is being polite."

Elizabeth mentioned Caroline Bingley with notable regularity. Darcy felt a ripple of pleasure at the prospect of her being jealous of that lady's attentions to him.

"Now," Elizabeth continued, oblivious, "I could not help but notice the manner in which you looked at your reflection yesterday, so I have taken the liberty of borrowing this for you." She held aloft a razor.

Darcy smiled broadly in gratitude for her simple yet vastly welcome bit of thoughtfulness. Once she had provided water, soap, and a mirror, and removed to her bedchamber that he might shave in private, he lathered his face and took up the razor. It took fewer than three attempts and more than as many nicks to his face to determine that his wound rendered him incapable of holding his head at the required angle. He tossed the razor down and pounded his fist on the table in vexation. He wished he had not when the noise brought Elizabeth hastening back to his side before he could rinse either the soap or the blood from his face.

"*Can you fetch the boy to assist me?*" he mouthed. "*John, is it?*"

"He is the innkeeper's nephew, not a valet." She said it gently, though Darcy still felt strangely admonished. "In any case, I do not believe he is yet shaving himself. I am not sure how much help he would be."

Darcy closed his eyes and let out a cautious sigh.

"Should you like me to do it?"

He looked at her sharply. "*Certainly not!*"

"Why not? It does not look to be all that difficult. Besides, technically, you have already had your throat slit. How much more damage could I possibly do?"

"*No!*" he insisted, vexed that his muteness made a mockery of his resolve. "*It would be insupportable.*"

Elizabeth grinned disconcertingly. "Come now, Mr Darcy. 'Tis not as though you have been asked to dance with me at a ball. *That* would truly be a punishment. *This* is merely a practicality."

Her grin notwithstanding, he felt certain she meant more by this than a passing jest. She spoke on, however, giving him no time to dwell on it.

"Nay, you are right, though. I think you ought to remain as you are, with that little bit bald"—she pointed at the part he had attempted to shave already—"and the rest *au naturel*, as God intended."

She was devilishly alluring when she was being teasing. So be it! Let the stubborn woman do as she pleased. They were a few weeks of recovery and a question away from being married anyway. All being well, they would be pursuing more improprieties than a paltry shave soon enough.

He indicated with a gesture and a small smile that she should proceed, and there passed an exceedingly enjoyable few minutes as Elizabeth laughed and joked her way through shaving the right side of his face. She leant close enough that he could feel the heat of her and see dozens of pale freckles across her nose and cheeks that he would wager bronzed delightfully in the summer. And to his vast pleasure, she appeared to have recalled, almost precisely, the outline of his side whiskers. Whether that meant she had paid closer attention to his countenance above any other or was just generally observant, he dared not suppose, but he knew which he wished to be true.

"What were you doing on the same road as me on the day of the accident?" she enquired out of the blue.

The answer was mortifying enough that Darcy flinched with chagrin. The razor slipped slightly, startling Elizabeth into adjusting her grip. Regrettably, her snatch for it only hastened the blade's trajectory, and it sliced into his cheek. She dropped it with a shriek and recoiled. Darcy unintentionally gasped, a sound that stuck in his throat and left him spluttering and gulping for breath.

"Forgive me!" Elizabeth begged over and over again, snatching up the face-cloth and dabbing at his bleeding cheek. "I should never have insisted upon doing it. Forgive me!"

After a slow, steadying breath, Darcy took her by her wrists and gently pulled her hands away from his face. *"A scratch, nothing more. It is well."*

"It is not well, sir. I have cut your face!"

Darcy glanced sidelong at his reflection. A small nick about an inch long ran just above his jaw line. He doubted it would even scar, but Elizabeth was evidently mortified regardless. He pointed at the several scrapes his attempt to shave the other cheek had left. *"As have I."*

"That is hardly the same; those are tiny."

"Being cut shaving is not uncommon."

She gave him a withering look. "Either that is a lie, or you are in dire need of a better manservant."

He only just recalled not to laugh aloud but smiled broadly and cautiously leant towards the table for the pen and paper.

I have had facial hair for longer than my present man has been in my employ.

Elizabeth read it then sank heavily into the nearest chair. "You are very good to try and ease my mind. It is not working, but I appreciate the effort."

It is in my interests. I need you to finish the job.

"Under no circumstances!" she exclaimed. "Look how my hands are shaking!"

You cannot leave me with half a beard!

"It is more like a quarter of a beard now. I daresay nobody will notice."

"*Elizabeth!*" he mouthed, beginning to enjoy the matter less—until she smiled and her whole face lit up.

"Very well," she conceded. "Only be sure not to wriggle this time. Nobody's looks are such that he requires his face be underscored *twice*."

Darcy sat as still as he was able while she worked, though his heart tripped over itself as he attempted to discern whether she had intended to flatter him. Nonetheless, he hoped she would finish soon, for his neck still throbbed mercilessly, and now the cut on his cheek stung too. As evasive manoeuvres went, sacrificing one's face was an excessive recourse, but he supposed it had spared him from the awkward admission of chasing Elizabeth about the country. He smiled to himself. All his recent injuries notwithstanding, Darcy was inordinately pleased to have caught up with her at last.

Confessions in the Dark

T he escapade proved disproportionately tiring, and Darcy slept for a good part of the rest of the day, not reawakening until dusk. He lay still, assessing his various aches and pains before attempting to move, but was distracted by the faint and infrequent sounds of rustling and tapping. As he turned his head on the pillow, something small sailed across the room and bounced across the table with a soft noise. He turned his head a little farther to where Elizabeth was slouched in one of the chairs, her elbow on the arm and her cheek resting in the palm of her hand. She lifted her head to rip a corner from the piece of paper in her lap—one of their messages to each other by the look of it—and roll it into a ball between her fingers. This she then threw at the table—nay, at the candle upon it, Darcy thought. It came close enough to make the flame dance sideways, but ulti-mately missed and skittered across the table to the floor as its predecessor had done. Elizabeth puffed out her cheeks and returned her head to her hand.

Though it was no bad thing that their written communications be destroyed, Darcy reflected ruefully that under better circumstances, were he to be trapped alone in a bedchamber for a week with Elizabeth, he should not like to think that she would be dull for one moment of it. He reached surrepti-tiously to slide another of their obsolete notes off the nightstand and quietly tore off a corner to make his own projectile. He threw it at the candle and, more by luck than judgment, hit it. Elizabeth whipped her head around to look at him in surprise. He let a small smirk tug at the corner of his mouth. She said nothing but inflicted a tug of a far more insistent nature upon him by slowly raising a solitary eyebrow. He swallowed, relieved that his bandages would disguise his discomposure, and mouthed, "*Your turn.*"

Elizabeth hit the candle only once and he thrice more before she declared the contest unfair. "You have the advantage lying there—you are at the better angle."

There was a pause while Darcy fought to suppress the temptation to suggest that she come and lie with him, after which he forced himself to get out of bed and into a chair and promptly proved Elizabeth correct by missing his next four shots.

"Let us stop," she said after the last. "It is evidently hurting you."

He did not object. The ache in his throat had worsened, and he did not think it was due to throwing a few trifling bits of paper. To detract from his own disquiet and the concerned manner in which Elizabeth peered at him, he wrote her a note.

I apologise for having been such poor company all week.

"You need not apologise," she assured him. "You have been very ill."

How have you passed the time?

"I have talked to the other guests, played cards with them once or twice, read a little." She grinned saucily and added, "I made a snowman."

This evidently delighted her, though whether she was better pleased by her own undertaking or his surprise, he would not have liked to say.

Was it a good one?

"No, not really. I got cold before I finished him, so he only had a belly and some arms. I called him Sir William."

Darcy's throat clamped closed around the laugh that bubbled up before he could prevent it, but as always, her wit took him by surprise, and she certainly had captured that man's two prevailing qualities: his paunch and his knight-hood. The resulting spasms deprived him of air for longer than was comfortable, and the joke had passed by the time he recovered himself. Nonetheless, he endeavoured to partake in her enjoyment.

I am sorry to have missed that. I have a talent for building snowmen of which I am unashamed to boast. My sister and I make it our business to build one together on the first snow of every winter.

"What a lovely thing to do," Elizabeth replied, sounding genuinely pleased, even if she looked a little surprised. "It is true, then, you *do* enjoy liveliness. I would never have believed it before this week. You did not betray any hint of it in Hertfordshire."

You did not see me in any places where liveliness was appropriate. It would be entirely impractical to build a snowman at a ball. Too many candles.

She laughed unrestrainedly at this—a sound that lifted Darcy's heart for knowing he had brought it about.

I am sorry you have had nobody with whom to build your snowmen. It must have been an exceedingly tedious few days. Would that I could have been awake for more of it.

She shook her head. "Truly, Mr Darcy, you must not concern yourself with that. You need to regain your strength, for Master John made it to Spencer's Cross this afternoon with our letters. The road on the far side of the village is still blocked, apparently, but he seems to think that as long as it does not snow again, it ought to clear within a day or two, and then the post can be delivered. It would be exceedingly vexing if, after all this, you were to keel over just as help arrived. You must concentrate on getting better."

"*I am better,*" he objected silently.

"I beg to differ."

He frowned and wrote,

Am I not sitting upright, conscious, and conversing?

"Barely." He must have reacted in some way for she winced sympathetically and made a placating gesture. "That is, you are certainly improving, but I would not say you are your usual self."

Darcy pulled a face of ambivalence. "*I am not sure I have ever been more at liberty to be myself.*" What was it that Elizabeth thought was different? And why was he now the object of such an intense look? "*What is it?*" he mouthed.

"Do you honestly like Miss Bingley?"

"*Pardon?*"

"You said the other day that she was not as awful as I thought. Do you *truly* think well of her?"

"*I do, yes.*"

"May I ask why?"

Fighting to repress the smile of triumph tugging at his lips, Darcy wrote,

May I enquire why it troubles you so much that I should?

"Because I cannot believe you actually enjoy her officious attention. I think I have discovered enough about your character to know you do not like to be so assiduously courted, yet you claim to esteem Miss Bingley, who I never saw do anything but speak and look and think for your approbation alone. I cannot account for it."

Darcy's complacency vanished. He ought to have known better than to think Elizabeth would be jealous of any woman—she must know she had no cause. No, it was *his* character she wished him to account for. Again.

I do not hold her in high regard because she fawns over me. I esteem her because she is refined.

Elizabeth screwed up her nose. "That is an absurd reason to admire some-one. You can like a person *more* for being refined, but you ought not to like them simply because of it, else you would like every well-dressed criminal in the country."

You asked me to justify my regard, and I have. Refinement is a quality I admire, whether or not you agree that I should.

"That is fair," she conceded with a modest smile and slight inclination of her head. "It is certainly not my intention to talk down Miss Bingley's merits. She has them, I am sure, and if you admire them, then that is all to the good. I only wished to establish whether your admiration was borne of vanity."

Are you convinced it is not?

After a brief pause and another searching look, she replied, "Yes." She almost sounded surprised, making Darcy uneasy.

It was no falsehood when you told Bingley you were a studier of character, was it? I have been questioned to within an inch of my life this past week.

She looked abashed and a little hurt, which had not been his intention, and he hastened to add,

By which I mean, I think it must be my turn.

"Do your worst, sir. I am not afraid of you."

Darcy fixed his gaze on her. *"You are not afraid of anything."*

He watched her watch his mouth as he said this but could not tell from her expression what she thought of it. She only lifted her eyes back to his and enquired, "What do you wish to know?"

He wished to know *everything* but thought it easiest to continue in the same vein in which they had already begun.

I know which traits you disdain — you have made certain I know your opinion
of such vices as vanity, pride, and resentment. Pray tell me, which qualities do
you admire?

Her head came up, and she answered, "Integrity," without hesitation, and something in the way she held his gaze made him feel no less under scrutiny than when she had been the one asking questions.

That is a fine quality indeed.

"And rarer than one might expect. Fortunately, it is not the sole measure of a good character, otherwise I should be perpetually disappointed."

He desperately wished to know who had disappointed her. Her friend, for marrying a fool? Bingley, for abandoning her sister? Him, for encouraging it? He was too cowardly to enquire and wrote, instead,

What else then? What other virtues are good enough to earn the good opinion
of the discerning Miss Elizabeth Bennet?

It would have been the height of vanity to ask the question in the hope of her answering with a list of qualities to match his own, and he assured himself that was not his design. Still, when she began by talking about her mother, he assumed her purpose was to chastise him by praising she whom he had unreservedly disparaged. Great was his chagrin as it dawned on him her answer had nothing in the slightest to do with him, no matter from which angle he viewed it.

Elizabeth spoke of Mrs Bennet in terms that had never occurred to Darcy. He had often seen her blush for her mother's behaviour and had never thought of the older woman in any other terms than as a source of embarrassment to the rest of her family. It was edifying, in a way that reflected very poorly on him, to hear Elizabeth speak proudly and tenderly of her mother's devotion to her family, her well-meant endeavours to do well by a husband and five children, each of vastly different temperaments, with limited means and an even more limited imagination at her disposal. Worldliness, refinement, intelligence—none of these things mattered to Elizabeth half as much as affection and goodness. Qualities the ostensibly unsophisticated Mrs Bennet apparently possessed in abundance.

It may not have been her object to humble him, but Darcy was nonetheless shamed. Why was it that every conversation with Elizabeth led to another facet of him being undone?

I must make an apology. I have grossly underestimated your mother if it is from
her that you have learnt your remarkable compassion.

She looked taken aback and even blushed a little. "Do not all mothers teach love and affection, by dint of loving us?"

He was not sure. His mother had given him good principles but spoilt him, he supposed, in not directing him more stringently on how he ought to follow them.

Elizabeth looked at him intently and bit off two attempts to speak before finally venturing, "Will you tell me about yours?"

Darcy baulked. He rarely talked about his mother.

My mother is dead.

Of course, his bluntness did not deter Elizabeth as it would most people— as it had been intended to do.

"I know that, sir," she replied softly. "She was still your mother."

He shifted in his seat, ignoring the way it pulled at the healing flesh upon his neck.

She has been dead a very long time.

"May I ask how long?" she enquired gently.

He opened and closed all five fingers of one hand three times to indicate that she had been dead these past fifteen years.

"So young."

Darcy knew not whether she referred to him or his mother so gave no response.

"She died birthing your sister?"

He replied in the negative with an extended finger and wrote,

A fever, unrelated. We never discovered the cause.

"And your sister an infant still?"

He touched the back of one hand with a finger of the other to confirm it.

"I am sorry. I imagine it was a dreadful time—for you and your father."

My father was away and unable to return in time. I held my mother's hand until she was gone. And for a day and a half afterwards.

He stared at the words, not knowing why he had written them. The only people who knew that tale were his housekeeper, Mrs Reynolds, and the long-deceased Mr Wickham Senior, Pemberley's steward at the time. It had been necessary for the latter to forcibly remove him from his mother's chamber, for he had refused to leave of his own accord. He dared not look up, for the admission made him feel intolerably exposed. He did not need to lift his eyes to see

Elizabeth lean forward to take the pen from his fingers and write beneath his last line,

That tells me all I could ever wish to know about your mother. Thank you.

He scowled furiously at the paper until he won the struggle to steady his belaboured breathing. Then he took the pen back.

Nay, I thank you. It is difficult to know what to say, for I recall very few details nowadays. My memories are mostly impressions now. I knew my father for longer.

"Was it necessary for you to sit with him also at the end?"

I had no time to sit. He was hale and hearty until the moment he suffered an apoplexy and dropped dead in front of me.

Elizabeth raised a hand to cover her mouth, and he might have felt bad for shocking her but for the expression in her eyes. He did not usually enjoy people's pity, but hers gave him greater comfort than he had felt in many years.

"How old were you when you lost him?" she enquired with the utmost tenderness.

He showed her on his fingers.

"Two and twenty? That is but a year older than I am now. I know not how I should cope being charged with responsibility for Longbourn, let alone a vast estate and any one of my younger sisters. It must have been terrifying."

The room was dark and cold and unfamiliar. It felt a thousand miles away from anything Darcy knew—as though no one would ever know if he made the confession that crouched, leaden, upon his tongue. He dipped the pen in the ink and wrote, slowly,

It still is.

He raised his eyes to hers. She said nothing but placed her hand over his and squeezed it. She may as well have taken hold of his heart and squeezed that.

"It is too easy to assume that wealth and privilege assure smooth waters. I daresay both your parents would be incredibly proud of you."

Never had he wanted to kiss her more—especially when a log collapsed in the fire, sending a plume of sparks and ash up the chimney and making her jump in fright, then laugh heartily at herself for it. He smiled indulgently at her, enjoying the glow the enlivened flames cast upon her countenance. The impulse to pull her into his embrace was so great he almost scrawled out a proposal there and then, and might have, had a wave of lightheadedness not sent any such fanciful notions scuttling from his mind.

"There, you see, you are not as well as you think," Elizabeth said, her amusement quashed by concern. "Perhaps you ought not to have sat up for this long."

Darcy thought he had sat up for longer yesterday but was not in any way to argue. Despite her urging, he declined any food but accepted her help to stagger back to the bed. A bubble of unease arose in his stomach when she touched her hand to his forehead. "*Fever?*" he mouthed.

"Nay, I think it is only that you are still weak. Go to sleep. I am sure you will feel better in the morning."

Darcy was sick of sleeping. He was sick of hurting, too. He wished to be better—strong again, and clean, and home—and married. Indeed, there was but one good thing to have come out of this entire damnable mess. He smiled at her as best he could with lips rendered unwieldy by exhaustion. *Would that my parents could have met you, sweetest Elizabeth. Then they would have been truly proud.* He closed his eyes, hoping that if he must sleep again, it would at least be punctuated with dreams of her.

Out in the Cold

Darcy slept ill, flitting close to the surface of full wakefulness too many times to receive any actual rest. When he struggled out of the cloying stupor, he was met with exhaustion. His throat hurt in a new way; myriad tiny pieces of glass embedded at the back of his mouth, scraping against his tongue every time he swallowed. Fog had returned to his head, and his face hurt. He sat up carefully, wincing against the daylight and perturbed to realise the lateness of the day. For how long had he slept?

Elizabeth was not there. He thought to relieve himself before she appeared but found he did not need to. He considered taking a few mouthfuls of leftover broth but found he had no appetite. Instead, he washed his hands and face in the cold water left on the nightstand and tottered unsteadily to the chair by the hearth to throw another log on the fire.

By the time it had burned black, he had grown distinctly vexed by Elizabeth's absence. She had not answered his knock at her bedchamber door, though the want of any noise from beyond it had already convinced him she was not within. He had stood at the window, watching until he could stand no longer, but there was no sign of anyone upon the snowy, wooded hillside it faced. He had drifted off, only to be awoken by the cramp in his neck that sleeping askew now guaranteed. What time was it now?

He moved to sit at the table and picked up the book Elizabeth had been reading. Tucked between the pages was his note confessing to finding her intimidating. Ordinarily, the discovery would have delighted him. At present, it only fuelled his displeasure. Why, if she cared to keep such a token, did she not care for the distress her unexplained absence would occasion him? Of course, there was no obligation for her to remain in this dingy, malodorous room with him, yet she had done so all week without complaint. Wherefore had she renounced his company today?

His hopes were roused when there came a knock at the door. It was not Elizabeth, though, for whoever it was then waited outside for permission to come in, as *she* had not done all week. Unable to give any command to enter, Darcy waited until he or she either went away or let themselves in. A few moments later, the young lad John opened the door and ambled towards the bed, presumably to collect the night spoils as he had at various other times that week. Darcy rapped his knuckles on the table to attract his attention.

"Beggar me and all me neighbours, who's there?" the boy shouted, jumping a foot in the air and looking wildly in all directions. He let out a great breath and thumped a fist to his chest upon espying Darcy. "Beggin' your pardon, sir. I thought no one was here."

Darcy waved away his concerns and mouthed, *"Have you seen Miss Bennet?"*

The boy only pulled a face.

"Miss Bennet," he repeated. He held an arm wide to indicate the empty room. *"My companion."*

"What's wrong with ya, mister? Can't you speak none?"

Darcy swore to himself and extended the forefinger of one hand to confirm that, no, he could not speak. He swore again when the boy looked quizzically in the direction his finger had pointed. Snatching up the pen, he dipped it in the well, flicking ink everywhere as he dashed off an explanation.

I cannot speak.

He held it up for John to read.

"Wishful thinking, that is, mister. I can't read no more than you can talk."

Darcy slapped the paper back onto the table and clenched his jaw. With a shrug, John walked to the bed, nudged the chamber pot with his toe, grunted at its emptiness, and walked back towards the door. Darcy opened his mouth to try once again to make himself understood and was incensed when the boy laughed.

"No hope, mister. No hope." With an irreverent nod, John was gone.

Darcy sat back in his chair and schooled himself to composure as he settled in to continue his vigil, for Elizabeth must return eventually, whether or not he paced the room until she did. What felt like days, but which his rational mind told him was more likely less than quarter of an hour later, he pushed himself to standing again. He gripped the back of his chair until the room ceased spinning, then walked to retrieve his boots from the corner in which they had stood redundant all week.

He anticipated that pulling them on would hurt, but the reality was worse.

As his frame went taut, every sinew in his neck twisted, his gullet convulsed, and his stomach lurched. A sputtering exhalation that ought to have been a shout of pain bubbled impotently in his throat. He dropped the boot and banged his fist on the table, willing himself not to vomit. He leant gingerly against the chair back and waited to see which would triumph, pain or impatience.

It was the latter. In all matters pertaining to Elizabeth, he had long tired of delay. Nevertheless, his determination cost him dearly, and by the time both boots were on, he was returned to wheezing like leaking bellows, and sweat slicked his brow. He wiped it away with his sleeve, struggled into his blood-stained waistcoat and left the room.

HE STEPPED OUT INTO A LANDING BOASTING SEVERAL OTHER DOORS, A TINY window, and a staircase. Assuming only bedchambers graced this floor, he headed in the direction of the stairs, at the foot of which he discovered the likely cause of a good number of his stranger delusions earlier in the week: a large stuffed bear, posed towering on its hind legs with an apple wedged in its snarling jaws. Beyond that antechamber, he came to a taproom, where a dozen tables were occupied by fewer than half a dozen people, not one of whom was Elizabeth.

"Well, I'll be, Mr Darcy!" From behind a counter on the opposite wall came a stooped, red-faced man wiping his hands on his apron. "What a fine thing to see you up and about! After the look of you when you first arrived, we had worried you would not survive the night."

Darcy winced at the indelicate allusion to his near-death, at the man's presumptuous familiarity, at the mortification of standing bloodied and unwashed before him, at the throbbing in his neck. All of it contributed to his exasperation, though none so much as Elizabeth's absence.

"Mr Timmins," the man added with a bow. "Proprietor and purveyor of fine ale, at your service."

"*Good day,*" Darcy mouthed.

"Ah, that is right—you cannot speak. Forgive me, Mr Darcy, your wife did tell us. And it is no wonder—nasty injury, that. Very nasty indeed."

But for a few blinks, Darcy held his countenance perfectly still. His heart was not so obedient and drummed out a dozen extra beats. His wife?

"Can I get you a drink, sir?" the man continued, oblivious.

"*No, I thank you. Have you seen—*"

"Come, have a seat."

Darcy ignored the man's attempts to usher him to an empty table. "*Have you—*"

"Would you like something to eat?"

"The man is trying to say something, Timmins. For God's sake, let him speak!" This welcome interruption came from a man whose crutch marked him as the lieutenant Elizabeth had mentioned.

Darcy sent him a nod of thanks, then wished he had not when pain erupted under his chin. Ignoring it as best he could, he mouthed, "*I am looking for Miss* —" He caught himself. "*Mrs Darcy.*"

In tandem, Timmins and Lieutenant Carver squinted at his lips, then shook their heads in incomprehension. Darcy mouthed it again, abhorring the spectacle he was making of himself.

"I do apologise, sir, but could you say it one more time, and more slowly—"

"He is obviously looking for Lizzy, Mr Timmins," said an elderly lady seated next to an even more ancient man at the next table over.

"Who?"

"His wife."

Someone by the fire with his back to the room scoffed derisively.

"Oh yes, of course!" Timmins said amiably. "I have not had the pleasure of seeing her today, sir. You might find her in the kitchen. Feel free to wander down and see for yourself. We have abandoned all ceremony this week, is that not right, Mrs Ormerod?"

"Quite so, Mr Timmins, quite so," replied the elderly lady. "It has been the perfect adventure."

Darcy made no response. He did not consider almost dying to be any shade of adventurous, and he was too pained to make head or tail of Timmins's strange suggestion. Having assumed Elizabeth had sought out some alternative company, a change of scene, or perhaps a different book, he had expected to be directed to another parlour, not the kitchen.

"Through there, down to the end and left," Timmins said, pointing to a door as he hobbled past it back to his counter. Thither Darcy would have gone, were it not for an unheralded wave of lightheadedness that left him doubting he could walk more than two steps without falling. He clutched discreetly at the back of the nearest chair to steady himself.

"Are you quite well, Mr Darcy?" Mrs Ormerod enquired. "You look uncommonly pale."

"Of course he is not well, dear," her husband answered. "Even my old eyes can see that. There is no need to embarrass him by drawing attention to it." To Darcy he said, "Pay her no mind, young man. You have been standing for longer than my hip will allow me."

"Or my leg me," said Carver. "It says much of our little company that a man whose head is only just still attached to his body is the halest among us."

"Happen she went to Spencer's Cross with Stratton."

Darcy looked sharply at the man sitting before the hearth, but he said no more and did not turn around.

"Aye, Mr Latimer, you might be right," agreed Timmins. "I know he meant to try and walk there this afternoon. Perhaps Mrs Darcy accompanied him."

Darcy stared hard at the floor, his throat announcing every breath as it hee-hawed in and out of him. Elizabeth had attempted the walk to the village again. After giving her word that she would not. Without so much as a note explaining where she had gone. In the sole company of a man whom she had known for less than a week. What was she thinking?

Latimer turned his head slightly to speak over his shoulder and down his nose. "Funny thing that, Mr Darcy. You not knowing where *your wife* is."

"There they are, coming along the road now," Timmins announced, nodding at a window to the front of the property. Through it, Elizabeth could clearly be seen walking ahead of Stratton, holding her skirts above the ankle as she every now and then broke into a run before being forced to walk again where the snow was deepest. Darcy needed to see no more. With more vigour than he truthfully had the strength for, but animated with outrage, he strode to the front door and wrenched it open.

The air was bitterly cold, and it instantly clasped its icy talons about his throat. In his pique, all the carefulness he had adopted to minimise his discomfort was forgotten. Every furious step sent shards of pain lancing from his chest to his chin until he could scarcely order his thoughts. He struck his boot on something hidden beneath the snow, instinctively took a jarring step to avoid falling, and fell to his knees anyway when a jolt of agony overtook him, making his vision swim.

"Oh my goodness! Darcy!" Elizabeth was on her knees beside him. "Can you hear me? Are you well?"

He gritted his teeth savagely and forced himself to answer in the affirmative with their agreed hand gesture.

Elizabeth hooked her hands under his arm and began to tug him up out of the snow. "What are you doing out here?"

Leaning more heavily on her than he liked, he pushed himself to his feet. "*Looking for you.*"

"Looking for…Are you out of your wits?"

"Mr Darcy, I presume?" At Stratton's arrival on the scene, Darcy instinctively jerked his arm tightly to his side, tugging Elizabeth closer with it. He made no attempt to conceal the resentful curl of his lip, even when, from the corner of his eye, he saw Elizabeth frown at him.

"Yes, this is he," she answered in his stead. "Pray excuse him, sir. He cannot speak"—she peered closer still—"and he is not well."

"*I am well enough,*" Darcy mouthed in retort. "*Do not apologise to this man for me.*"

Elizabeth recoiled, snatching her hands from his arm, her frown changed from one of concern to one of confusion and displeasure.

"Everything well out here? Uncle Timmins sent me to see if I can help any?" came an insouciant interruption from John, who was trotting towards them from the inn.

Darcy could scarcely contain his pique, for had the boy made more effort to help half an hour ago, he might not have ended up on his knees in the snow. *"Not now,"* he mouthed angrily.

"Yes, thank you, John. You could take this indoors for me," Elizabeth said, retrieving a basket from the snow and handing it to him. He took it with another of his shrugs and went away. *A boy of few words and even fewer manners,* Darcy reflected with disgust.

Turning to the other gentleman, Elizabeth said, "I thank you for your kindness this afternoon, sir. Pray, do not let me keep you from your wife a moment longer."

Stratton looked uneasily between her and Darcy, apparently unsure whether or not to leave. Darcy helped him shed his ambivalence by mouthing, severely, *"Good day, sir."*

"Good day, then," Stratton said with a conspiratorial look to Elizabeth that did nothing to soften Darcy's opinion of him. "Do be sure to let me know if there is any way in which Mrs Stratton or I can be of assistance."

Elizabeth assured him she would and remained silent as he walked away. The moment they both disappeared inside, Darcy turned, his lips already forming around his first question, but Elizabeth took full advantage of his muteness and spoke over him.

"What do you mean, being so uncivil to poor Mr Stratton?"

"Poor Mr Stratton?" Darcy repeated, incredulous.

"Aye, poor Mr Stratton! For what has he done to deserve your disdain? Or Master John? Do you *truly* think so meanly of the rest of the world that you cannot even *pretend* to be polite?"

"You would have me affect civility towards a man from whom you were just running away?" He enunciated as clearly as vexation allowed, but he could tell from the way she glowered at his lips that she did not comprehend. *"You were running from him,"* he mouthed instead, pointing angrily at the road along which she had just hurried.

Elizabeth looked where he pointed, then back to him in furious astonishment. "I was not running away from Mr Stratton—I was hastening back to *you!*"

"You were?"

"Yes, to see whether you were still alive!"

"If you were so concerned about me, why go at all? Without even a note! You must have known how I would worry."

The hiatus to which he had grown accustomed each time he gave a mute answer and she industriously struggled to understand it felt tortuous in this new context of dispute. Her tone, when she replied, suggested a loss of equanimity that justified his anxious wait.

"You were babbling deliriously when you fell asleep yesterday. You tossed and turned all night long and then could not be woken this morning, no matter how I tried. I had serious doubts as to whether you would survive the day. Waking up, reading a letter, and coming for a stroll outside were not things of which I suspected you capable when I left in urgent search of an apothecary. I see now that I need not have been concerned at not finding one. You evidently require no medical attention whatsoever, for your pride, at least, is in fine fettle."

Part of Darcy wished to crow at the news that Elizabeth had been so troubled by the prospect of his demise. A greater part of him railed at yet another attack upon his character. "*I misjudged. That scarcely makes me prideful.*"

"No? You did not then presume that Mr Stratton's condition in life meant he could never be respectable?"

"*You do not know that he is.*"

"I do not know that *you* are, yet I have been alone with you all week and have heard no complaint from you about that."

"*You have nothing to fear from me,*" he replied indignantly.

"But I do have something to fear from him? Why? Because I told you he is in trade and now you think him vulgar?"

Darcy snarled derisively. "*He thought it proper to walk eight or nine miles with you, unaccompanied. What says that about his respectability?*"

"He did not choose to walk anywhere with me," she cried. "I walked there alone, as did he, and when our paths crossed, he kindly accompanied me back."

Darcy stared at her in consternation. "*You went alone? After you gave me your word you would not? Devil take it, Elizabeth, you do not know the area. It was not safe!*"

She squinted furiously at his mouth but could only have caught one in four of his words, for he was exasperated well beyond measured speech. However many she deciphered, it seemed to be enough.

"I am well aware of that, Mr Darcy, but I thought you were gravely ill. Would you rather I had left you to die?"

"*I would rather you had sent someone else.*"

She shook her head. "The only people I might have prevailed on are Mr Stratton and Master John. One had gone there already before I even resolved on going myself and would not have known to look for an apothecary. The other was at his work, helping his uncle. What was I to do? Demand that they both desist and do my bidding instead? These people are not in my employ, sitting about awaiting my instructions."

"*It would not have hurt them to do you a small favour.*"

"Upon my word, think you they have not done enough already? John walked to Spencer's Cross only yesterday, if you recall, through far deeper drifts than still remained today, to deliver our letters—which have been collected now, it transpires, so you may thank him for that." She began to walk back and forth before him, gesturing angrily as she spoke. "He has also, in case it has somehow escaped your notice, been emptying our chamber pots all week. Think you that is his job? Mr Timmins has been caring for your horse. Mrs Ormerod and Mrs Stratton have helped me wash and shred linens to dress your wound. Indeed, they have all done quite enough! I have two perfectly good legs of my own—why would I *not* walk to the village myself?"

Her words sounded odd. Darcy worried for a moment she was weeping but recognised at the last it was not tears that shook her voice. Her teeth were chattering. Which was strange, for he no longer felt cold at all. All he felt was escalating resentment at Elizabeth's obstinate irascibility towards him.

"*I am very grateful to all of them,*" he mouthed. "*I was only concerned for you, madam. You are cold. We had better go in.*" Without waiting for her, he turned and walked in that direction.

"I rather think you were concerned for *yourself,*" she said behind him.

He stopped walking, arrested by indignation and held in place by the prodigious effort of remaining upright despite his vertiginous light-headedness.

"You are angry because I did not leave you a note or heed your wish that I not walk to the village. You are too used to having your own way, Mr Darcy—but you have no right to be angry with me. I am wholly unconnected to you and am under no obligation to please you."

He whirled around, the injury to his neck wrenching nauseatingly and the spinning in his head taking longer to come to a stop than he did. He could not guess her purpose in goading him. Did she mean to upbraid him for not having proposed yet? It was a cruel ruse, given her presumption in announcing it to everybody else. "*True,*" he replied, ensuring he mouthed the words clearly, that she not miss a single one. "*Yet, though you disdain my solici-tude and constantly challenge my integrity, you had no scruple in telling everybody you are my wife!*"

Elizabeth gave a despairing and utterly humourless laugh. "I told nobody anything. They heard me call you *Mr* Darcy when we arrived, then I attended to you all through that first night, and by the next morning, they had begun calling me *Mrs* Darcy. What was I supposed to do—tell them we are *not* married? Frankly, sir, I was too busy trying to keep you alive to trouble myself with what anybody thought."

He gritted his teeth, vexed beyond measure that every attempt to justify himself only made him sound more churlish. He opened his mouth to apolo-gise, but Elizabeth spoke first, and her words silenced him far more effectively than the horse who kicked him had.

"You must not be anxious, though. You are quite safe from me. You had almost convinced me, this week, that my first impression of you was wrong—that the arrogance, the conceit, and the selfish disdain of the feelings of others that you displayed in Hertfordshire were not a true reflection of your charac-ter. But one foray out of your sick bed, and you have betrayed all the same pride and contempt as you did then…and I begin once again to think it must be true."

Each accusation hit him harder, winded him more. "*That what must be true?*"

"Mr Wickham's account of your dealings with him."

Darcy did go cold then, though inside, not out. Wickham! *"What has he told you?"*

"Everything."

"I doubt that."

"He told me that you have reduced him to his present state of poverty. Withheld the advantages designed for him, deprived the best years of his life of that independence which was no less his due than his dessert. But if there is more, pray enlighten me!"

Darcy could only stare. There was too much to feel for him to settle on anything; his head and his heart both reeled. He knew, from their many and intimate conversations that week, that Elizabeth was familiar with the worst of his faults. Nonetheless, he had thought she understood him. She had allowed him, encouraged him even, to believe she admired those other parts of him he had revealed. Now she told him *this* was the estimation in which she held him!

"This is your opinion of me? After all we have discussed this week, how could you think it of me?"

She wilted a little. He might even have thought her expression was one of concern, had she not just emphatically renounced any possibility of regard for him.

"I do not wish to believe it, for I truly had begun to think better of you. But when I observe you with my own eyes behaving in this way towards people —*good* people, undeserving of your contempt—when you are so imperious in your manner towards me, it is difficult *not* to believe you could have behaved similarly towards Mr Wickham. Even if you have then justified it to yourself under some imaginary act of friendship, as you did when you separated Mr Bingley and Jane."

Furious words he wished to hurl at her wedged instead against the constriction in Darcy's gullet. He choked on them, noisily and painfully, for several moments before he was able to gasp a breath. Elizabeth stepped forwards with her hands out towards him, but her conflicted expression only provoked Darcy to wave her away. He had never asked for her assistance, and if she meant to bestow it so unwillingly, he would have no more of it. *"Save your attentions for Wickham,"* he mouthed resentfully. *"With misfortunes as great as you describe, he will have more need of your compassion."*

All the concern vanished from Elizabeth's countenance, replaced with outrage. "There, you see? What am I to conclude when you treat the mention of his misfortunes with contempt and ridicule?"

"That you are a far worse studier of character than you believe."

"Lizzy! Mr Darcy! Do come inside. Lieutenant Carver has rustled up some soup with the bits Lizzy brought from the village." A woman whose acquaintance Darcy had yet to make waved as she picked her way through the snow towards them.

"Go away!" Darcy wished to rail at her, but Elizabeth was watching him, the severe line of her mouth and single raised eyebrow leaving him in no doubt that she waited, without much hope of a good performance, for his response, and he was loath to oblige her.

"Oh, but you are not well, sir!" the woman said upon reaching them. "Take him upstairs directly, Lizzy. I shall send John up with a tray for you both."

"There is no need, Mrs Stratton," Elizabeth replied with forced gaiety. "He sounds awful, I know, but Mr Darcy is recovered enough to have come all this way in search of me and hold a remarkably *lively* conversation. I am quite sure he is up to sitting on a chair in the parlour for a short while, and I daresay he will benefit from the society."

Despite everything, the look of challenge she then threw him still stole Darcy's breath away. Mrs Stratton said something about the evils of being confined to one place for too long, but he could scarcely concentrate on it past the combined distractions of his simmering indignation, the ringing in his ears, the cold in his feet, and Elizabeth's expectant stare. Doing his utmost to remain vertical, he offered Mrs Stratton his arm. A heartbeat or two after he set out towards the inn with her, he heard Elizabeth's feet crunching in the snow as she fell in behind them.

A Lesson, Hard Indeed

Wickham! As though he had not caused enough damage already, the malingerer had now set his sights on Elizabeth? The cur's purpose, Darcy was convinced, could only have been to cause *him* the utmost pain, for Elizabeth was too poor ever to be of real interest to such a man. Damn him—and damn her, too, for believing him!

"Here you are, Mr Darcy, warm yourself on this." A steaming bowl of soup was pushed into his field of view, and a small roll dropped next to it, which shed a faint cloud of flour as it bounced on the table.

How strong was their attachment? It galled Darcy to consider what nature of sentiment Wickham must have created to inspire such loyalty, for Elizabeth had spent this entire week in *his* company, discussing all manner of personal confidences, yet was still persuaded to believe whatever version of events the fiend had related.

"Pray, be not offended, Lieutenant Carver," Elizabeth said testily. "I believe we may infer Mr Darcy's gratitude from the manner in which he is staring at the food."

"'Tis well, madam. We all know your husband cannot speak."

Darcy looked up to discover himself the cynosure of all eyes in the room. Most were only curious; Elizabeth's were accusing. He swore to himself, for it had been his intention to prove her wrong about his manners, not make the damned case for her.

"*Thank you, sir,*" he mouthed to the lieutenant.

Carver inclined his head. "You are welcome, though I am no more after thanks and praise than your lovely wife has been all week. 'Tis a meal shared between friends, that is all." He began to eat, as did everybody else.

Darcy's gaze drifted back to the bowl before him, but his appetite had long since fled. "Reduced him to his present state of poverty, indeed!" he thought bitterly as he ripped his roll in two. The audacity of the lie was as staggering as the inaccuracy of it. *No less his due than his dessert?* What Wickham believed had proved manifestly out of kilter with reality. *No more after thanks and praise than your lovely wife…*

Replaying the words caught his attention as they had not when Lieutenant Carver spoke them aloud. He placed both halves of his roll down on the table and turned to regard Elizabeth. She must have noticed, for his injury required him to twist his entire frame in her direction, yet she did not acknowledge his attention. He began to feel more than commonly anxious as he reflected on her observation several days prior that the broth they had supped together could do with more salt—and that of the broth which she had brought him the following day being saltier. "You might find her in the kitchen," Timmins had said. Elizabeth's cheeks pinked under his continued gaze, but still she did not look up, and Darcy knew then, with abysmal certainty, that she had been cooking his food all week. While he lay abed bemoaning any prolonged absence from his side.

"It is very good, Carver," Latimer said with a mouthful. "Though I own I do long for a good beef steak."

A low rumble of accord rolled around the room. Darcy's head began to throb. How was he to know she had acted as servant all week, for she had said nothing of it!

"I used to like snow," said Mrs Ormerod. "But I shall not be sorry if I never see another flake."

"No, nor I," replied Mrs Stratton. "The novelty of making do has most definitely begun to wear off. I should very much like to go home."

"I spoke to a Mr McGregor in the village, dear," her husband informed her. "He is of the opinion the roads ought to clear in a day or two. Merryweather will be back with the carriage as soon as may be."

"I understand you have sent word to your cousin, also, Mr Darcy?"

Darcy lifted his gaze to Lieutenant Carver's and mouthed, "*I have.*"

"And that he is in the army?"

"*He is.*"

"What regiment, might I enquire? Might be as I know him."

He sincerely doubted Carver would be acquainted with an officer of Fitzwilliam's rank, but was sufficiently curious as to be willing to find out. Elizabeth forestalled him, however.

"Oh, he moves about far too often for us to keep track of him," she said airily. "We have long since given up attempting it."

Darcy looked askance at her. She returned his glance with a subtle but expressive look and extended one finger in their established signal for no. She did not wish that he reveal Fitzwilliam's identity? The fog in Darcy's head made it uncommonly difficult to attend to reasoning why. He supposed, were Fitzwilliam to be known to Carver, then his own identity as master of Pemberley would soon after be confirmed. His gut knotted. She wished that the tale of Fitzwilliam Darcy and Elizabeth Bennet's incarceration together not be revealed to the world. For which there could be but one explanation: she would avoid any possibility of being forced to marry him.

He returned his gaze to the table. Notwithstanding the revelation that she believed Wickham's tales of woe, still it dismayed him to discover the degree of her antipathy to the union.

"That is often the case," Carver replied, oblivious to their private exchange. "It can be an itinerant occupation and lonely as a consequence."

"Precisely why I opted for innkeeping," Timmins piped up. "Society comes to *me* this way and is generally too thirsty by the time it arrives to object to this." He waggled his right shoulder up and down to indicate the unnatural curvature of his spine.

"My father desired that I go into the navy," Mr Ormerod croaked. "I preferred the church. There seemed to me much less chance of getting wet."

Darcy sneered at his soup. His own father had intended that George Wickham should be awarded a living in the church. Would that the work-shy reprobate had gone to sea instead; considerable misfortune might have been avoided.

"Your young man has a most forbidding countenance, Lizzy."

He gritted his teeth. No doubt he had not been meant to hear this whispered remark from Mrs Ormerod, leant almost out of her chair to make the observation to Elizabeth—but he had, and it soured his temper further still. He was in no humour to perform to this motley assembly of strangers. And he was not 'Elizabeth's man.'

"You must not be afraid of him, Mrs Ormerod," Elizabeth replied in a voice evidently intended that he should hear. "He has a severe mien, but he is not *at all* above his company. If he were able to speak, I am sure he would charm you all with his easy conversation and inviting manners."

"I am not surprised to hear it, my dear, for you are so like that yourself," the old lady replied. "And, in fairness, I imagine he is still in a good deal of pain. Anybody so seriously injured has a right to look as displeased as he does."

Darcy would have given his left arm to lie down. His head swam in such a way as threatened to drown every thought—though his indignation was more than sufficiently buoyant that he chafed at Elizabeth's veiled reproof. He had never excelled at catching the tone of people's conversation or appearing interested in their concerns, as he often saw done. That did not make him disagreeable; it made him a man of few words.

He attempted prodigiously hard to ignore the recollection of having made the same observation, in a less charitable light, of John but a quarter of an hour earlier.

"We are an odd mix, are we not?" Timmins said. "An innkeeper, a soldier, an actor, a merchant, and a clergyman. I expect I could find a joke in amongst that lot somewhere, were there no ladies present. Pray, Mr Darcy, what is your profession?"

A curt and derisive laugh came from the seat by the fire. "You may surmise, from that look, that you have mortally offended him, Timmins," Latimer drawled. "Mr Darcy is evidently not a man with an *occupation*."

"A gentleman then," Timmins replied. "But you are not offended, are you, sir?"

"How strange that you think he would be," Elizabeth interjected. "Being high-born does not predispose Mr Darcy to regard with contempt anyone whose situation in life differs from his own."

Every stroke with which she defended Wickham galled Darcy more, and he responded heatedly. *"Neither does inferior birth predispose anybody to probity."*

"What did he say?" Mr Ormerod enquired.

Elizabeth concealed her pique well; Darcy fancied only he might observe the steely glint in her eyes or how very still she held herself as she answered with affected indifference, "Oh, he agreed with me that every person ought to be judged by the same standards, regardless of descent."

"Quite right," said Stratton. "I see many types of people in my shop, and I can assure you, 'tis manners, not money, that maketh man."

"Manners can be misleading," Darcy mouthed, looking at Elizabeth. *"People often put too much sway in charm and good looks."*

"What was that?" Stratton asked.

"He said people ought not to be judged on their appearance alone," Elizabeth explained icily. "With which I could not agree more. Think of how many fewer ladies would be slighted at balls if men could be tempted to give consequence to those who were only tolerably handsome."

It took a long moment, and Elizabeth watched him piercingly the whole while, but eventually the fog in Darcy's head lifted sufficiently that the pertinent memory surfaced. The first evening that ever he laid eyes upon her, he had spurned an introduction on the basis of her insufficient looks. He had been perfectly aware she was within earshot when he said as much, too. It had been his design to erase all expectation, to spare himself the indignity of dancing with a stranger. It seemed he had done far better: he had erased all expectation of any manner of connexion whatsoever. Marrying him could not be farther from Elizabeth's mind, in which he had apparently fixed himself as an ill-tempered, ill-mannered creature from the very first moment of their acquaintance. And in doing so, he had all but secured Wickham's place in her heart as the natural foil to his own irascible incivility. He suppressed the groan that would only choke him were he to allow it voice and opened his mouth to apologise, but it was all far too late.

"Pray, excuse me, I am tired after my walk to the village. I should like to lie down for a while." Elizabeth pushed her chair back noisily and stood up from the table. When Darcy made to do likewise, she waved him back into his seat. "You had far better stay here. I mean to rest. I would be no company for you at all." She thanked Carver for the meal, sent a wan smile in the direction of the other ladies, and left without another word.

"'Tis little wonder Mrs Darcy is tired," said Mr Stratton to nobody in particular. "It was not an easy walk to Spencer's Cross."

"I must say, I am surprised she went so far," Mrs Ormerod said in another of her indelicate asides.

"She was hoping to find an apothecary for Mr Darcy," Stratton replied awkwardly, sending him an apologetic look. Darcy forced himself to smile in acknowledgement.

"Ah yes," Mrs Ormerod said to him directly, abandoning all semblance of discretion. "She has been excessively concerned for you this week, sir."

Darcy was acutely aware of everybody's attention—his own rasping breath accentuated their silent wait for his answer—yet he knew not how to reply. Elizabeth thought him arrogant, prideful, and ungracious. She believed him capable of wilfully and wantonly throwing off the companion of his youth, of ruining the immediate prosperity and blasting the prospects of her apparent favourite George Wickham. She had called him out for egregiously ungentleman-like behaviour. How concerned could she truly be for a man she held in such poor esteem?

He swallowed painfully. Concerned enough to walk to this place that first day, through a snowstorm, to secure him aid, then return with the men to fetch him. Concerned enough to have risked her reputation to singlehandedly and bloody-mindedly nurse him back from death's door. Concerned enough to walk out again today in search of further assistance.

Looking at nobody in particular, he mouthed, *"She is exceptionally compassionate."*

That was why he loved her.

"What was that?"

"Did you catch what he said?"

"I cannot comprehend a word that passes his lips!"

"I must say," Stratton remarked over the plethora of questions, "I cannot blame her for having been anxious. If you will pardon me, Mr Darcy, you do look rather ill."

"Hush now," his wife replied. "Lizzy said he is well, and she knows him best."

"I agree with Mr Stratton," Carver opined, sidling awkwardly into Elizabeth's vacant chair. "You look decidedly unwell, sir."

Darcy *felt* unwell, though whether his injury or his conscience were responsible was difficult to discern. Mrs Stratton was right; Elizabeth did know him. He had accused her of being a poor studier of character, but of course, that entirely missed the point. Studying characters was precisely what she did—and what she had been doing. Rather than blithely accept Wickham's account of him, she had spent the better part of a week questioning him, that she might judge for herself. If she had still found him wanting, could he justly lay any blame at Wickham's door?

"You've not touched your soup, either," Carver observed.

Darcy grimaced weakly and mouthed, "*Not hungry.*" Without much forethought, he added, "*Has she been cooking for everyone?*"

Carver peered closely at his lips. "Cooking for everyone?" When Darcy confirmed that had been his question, the lieutenant's expression softened to one of surprising sympathy. "I see you are worried, but there is no need. We've not taken advantage. With Timmins's sister being snowed out, and him being about as good a cook as I am a dancer, we've mostly dined on his bread and cheese—and meat and fruit 'til that ran out. *You* could not swallow, though, by all accounts. It was my understanding that your wife prepared something less likely to finish you off than a great hunk of cheddar. She was good enough to share it with the rest of us each time she made more."

Darcy sighed heavily. The sound it made caused him to feel bilious and a deep frown to crease across Carver's brow. "*Thank you for clarifying, Lieutenant. And I apologise for ruining your shirt.*"

Carver's face made obvious his incomprehension, and Darcy lifted an elbow and tugged his sleeve to indicate the article of clothing to which he referred.

"Ah! Do not you worry about that, sir," came the reply. "A shirt is neither here nor there when a man's life is in the balance. It really was a most unfortunate accident. We are all delighted to see you recovered."

Darcy was unaccustomed to such easy camaraderie with strangers. He wondered briefly if his incapacity, or perhaps his present anonymity, might have occasioned it, but he could not fool himself for long. It was Elizabeth they all esteemed, and him only by association.

"*Excuse me,*" he mouthed. "*I must go to Eliz... I must go.*" He stood up—and sat back down again heavily as the room whirled about him in great, stomach-churning revolutions.

"Good Lord, steady on, sir!"

More than one voice asked whether he required assistance but in response to them all, he gave the silent lie that he was well. When the room ceased spinning, he pushed himself more cautiously to his feet, mouthed a general thank you to everyone present, and walked unsteadily from the room.

An Unkind World

Darcy could have sworn the damned bear growled at him as he passed it. Mayhap it was only his own hoarse breathing. Mayhap he was losing his mind. It felt that way—he could make sense of nothing. There were twice as many stairs going up as there had been coming down, and he was exhausted by the time he reached the landing. He did not pause to catch his breath, for such he had not successfully managed since Tuesday last in any case, and instead he strode directly to knock upon the door adjacent to his. There was no answer. He knocked again. Silence.

Would that he could speak, plead to be heard, for the need to lessen her ill opinion, by even the smallest margin, weighed unbearably heavy on him. He knocked a third time and listened so hard it was a wonder he could not hear woodworm chewing the beams—but of Elizabeth, he heard not a murmur. Surely she was above pretending to be absent to avoid him? A flurry of alarm churned his stomach, and he gave propriety little more than a passing thought as he opened the door to look for her.

She was not within, which was not surprising for it was instantly obvious this was not her bedchamber. A man's clothes lay strewn across an unmade bed. Several Hessian boots, none of which matched each other, were dotted about the floor. An open bottle of liquor stood on the nightstand, and an unemptied chamber pot took pride of place on a chair in the centre of the room.

Darcy backed out and peered along the landing. On this side of the building, there were only two doors. He walked to the other and opened it—his

chamber. He walked back to the first and looked inside again—still not Elizabeth's. He returned to the landing and stared at the wall betwixt the two where
the door to her room ought to have been but was not. He knew not what to
make of it.

Feeling somewhat detached from proceedings, he returned to his own
chamber and knocked instead on the connecting door to the room in which
Elizabeth had been sleeping all week. Again, there was no answer and, half
expecting to walk into the dream world of earlier in the week, filled with
murderous bears and drunken Bingleys, he opened this door as well. He was
greeted with no such sight and came up short. He groaned, then choked on it.

He had believed, when Elizabeth dried her hair before his fire, that she had
done so as a consequence of her easiness in his company. His vanity truly
knew no bounds. She had done so only for a want of her own fireplace. For
this was no separate bedchamber with adjoining door. This was but a small
storage room, lined on both sides with long, deep shelves piled high with all
the accoutrements of innkeeping. The bottom right shelf had been emptied and
arranged with a few blankets into a bed. Darcy closed his eyes and attempted
to order his miasmic thoughts. This was all exceedingly bad, though he knew
not which was worse: that Elizabeth had been sleeping in a cupboard, or that
she was not presently in it.

He turned on his heel and walked—slower than he would like but faster
than good sense told him was wise—back to the stairs, which he descended
leaning heavily against the bannisters. With gritted teeth, he pushed away
from the bottommost newel post and walked towards the taproom. He saw
before he entered that she had not returned there. He looked beyond those still
seated within to the windows that overlooked the road. Surely to God she had
not walked out again? Assuming not, he veered through the door to the back
of the inn. He made his way down an ill-lit passageway with his hands out
against both walls for balance, wary of every jutting flagstone lest it trip him
and jar his neck—until he heard Elizabeth's plea, whereupon all awareness of
his injury evaporated.

"Let me pass, sir. Nay, I insist you let me pass!"

Darcy strode towards her voice. She was in the kitchen, backed against a
worktable with a jug clutched desperately to her chest. Mr Latimer loomed
before her, too close to have anything but wickedness on his mind. Unable to
shout, Darcy hammered his fist against the nearest surface to announce his
presence. It frightened Elizabeth more than it did Latimer. She shrieked and
dropped the jug, sending water and shattered earthenware skittering across
the floor; he only glanced to see who it was, sneered, then turned back to his
prey.

"Go away, Darcy. This is none of your business."

"He is my husband!" Elizabeth cried, her evident attempt to sound indig-
nant lost beneath the tremble in her voice.

Latimer laughed at her. "No, he is not. Not unless you have pawned your ring. Besides, I spoke to your man, Rogers, the night you arrived. He didn't know this prig from Adam."

Elizabeth sent Darcy a look of sheer panic, but he had already seen and heard enough. He stepped forward, his arm extended to force Latimer aside and allow Elizabeth egress, but the man would not budge. He shoved Darcy's arm away and snarled an obscene directive for him to leave. Despite a thousand tiny stars filling his vision with white light, Darcy gave no ground. He held his arm out again, this time taking Elizabeth by the elbow and guiding her towards him.

"Get off!" Latimer growled, grabbing for her.

Darcy whipped around—something beneath his bandages strained and popped grotesquely—and bared his teeth at Latimer. And with rage roaring in his veins, there he remained, still and silent, glaring savagely until the cur's bravado visibly wilted.

"She does not even like you, you mute bastard," Latimer muttered—a parting rebuke that cut far deeper than he could ever imagine as he slunk into the shadows.

Darcy turned away, put his arm gently around Elizabeth's shoulders, and led her from the room.

"THANK YOU," SHE WHISPERED.

It was too dim to bother mouthing anything in response, and Darcy was, in any case, too distracted attempting to navigate the passageway to hold a conversation. His shoulder brushed a protruding brick, unbalancing him, and he stumbled slightly. He braced himself against the wall to keep from falling.

"Mr Darcy?"

The concern in Elizabeth's voice and a clatter from the kitchen gave him motivation aplenty to gather his wits and resume walking. Neither said any more as they walked past the taproom door and the dancing bear, up towards the landing. Only when Elizabeth cried out and clutched suddenly at his arms did Darcy become aware that he was moving in the wrong direction on the stairs. He had meant to be ascending, not swaying precariously backwards. He grabbed for the balustrade and gripped it fiercely until he regained his footing.

"You are not well," Elizabeth said, her hands still upon him as though convinced he would fall. He stared at them, savouring their warmth through his shirt sleeve and vaguely disgusted that the only way he seemed able to secure her tender touch was to hurl himself down a staircase. He stared too long; she withdrew her hands, leaving two spots of cold on his arm.

"I am sorry you had to—"

He cut her off with a sharp gesture and mouthed, *"Not your fault."* He would not listen to her apologise for Latimer's appalling indiscretion. With one hand still gripping the handrail, he placed his other on the back of her elbow, set his jaw, and escorted her the rest of the way to his room. Once inside, he walked her to a chair by the fireplace and gestured for her to sit, which she did without objection.

"Will you not sit down as well?" she enquired quietly.

"*In a moment,*" he mouthed. First, he lit the two candles on the table. Then he knelt to feed the dwindling fire. He stared overlong at the flames; when he stood up and walked to the bed, orange flickers danced before his eyes.

"What are you doing?" Elizabeth asked. "You will make yourself even more unwell."

He gathered the blanket from the bed into his arms and returned to her, holding it out like a shawl. "*I would make sure you are not cold.*"

Her eyes widened slightly, and she made a little noise, but said nothing, which Darcy took as permission to place the blanket about her shoulders. As he did so, his eyes fell to a rip in her dress. Beneath the rent in the fabric was a ghastly black bruise. His horror must have been plain to see, for Elizabeth followed his gaze in alarm, though she did not remain uneasy for long.

"Oh." She pulled the blanket tighter around her shoulders, covering the injury. "That was not Mr Latimer. I mean, he must have torn my dress, but the bruise is from the accident."

Darcy could only stare in abject dismay. "Nothing broken," she had assured him when he asked if she was hurt. Her damned carriage had overturned—how had he thought she might evade injury? He looked at the floor and winced. What a fine example of the selfishness of which she had accused him.

"It is not as bad as it looks," she said softly. "All bruises darken as they age. I can assure you, yours is worse."

He opened his mouth to speak but could find no words to say. They were all hidden in the fog coiling through his mind. He rubbed a hand over his face as he tried to straighten his thoughts.

"Truly, I wish you would sit down, sir. I think you are very ill."

He waved her concern away and looked about for the pen and paper. There, on the nightstand. He crossed the room to get them, but somehow stumbled into the bed and lurched forward onto his hands.

"Come, you had better lie down," Elizabeth said next to him. Her small, gentle hands were back on his arm as she tried to help him. Her tenderness was gut-wrenching, for Darcy knew now that it was naught but charity that bade her treat him thus. He extended a finger; he did not wish to lie down. "*Must tell you.*" He pushed himself away from the bed and reached for the inkwell, only to miss it as he swayed too far and staggered a step sideways.

"Let me then." Elizabeth collected up the writing equipment, and after a glance to ensure he was following, she returned to the table.

It felt good to be seated. For a moment, Darcy ceased fighting the intolerable fatigue bearing down upon him. He jerked back to awareness when the bear from the hall knocked on the door. He looked about the room in bewilderment. No bear—only Elizabeth regarding him with a deeply troubled expression. He licked his cracked lips and reached to dip the pen in the ink.

I am profoundly sorry that I was not more considerate of your well-being after the accident.

His hand felt numb and clumsy, and his writing suffered for it, but he thought it mostly legible and so twisted it around for Elizabeth to read.

She shook her head. "You need not apologise for that—you were half dead! And what could you have done anyway?"

The pen was dipped and poised to write that he could have comforted her, as she had him, before Darcy recalled she had no wish for any consolation he could give her. Ignoring the very real ache he felt in his chest for the loss of an entirely imagined connexion, he forced himself to write something else instead.

Unless I were actually dead, there could be no excuse for having paid so little attention to all that you have endured this week.

She leant to read as he wrote and began speaking before he finished. "If you mean my boiling up a little broth, I hardly think—"

She faltered when he extended a finger to contradict her. "What then?"

He pointed at the door to her 'bedchamber.' She looked thither also, then down at her hands in embarrassment.

Why?

He pushed the note to the edge of the table in front of her until she looked at it.

"This was the only room available," she answered dispiritedly. "It is Mr Timmins's sister's room. That is her store cupboard."

Darcy dipped the pen in the ink and underlined his previous question.

Elizabeth sighed deeply. "As I said, people assumed we were married. That did not mean we were obliged to share a bed."

Darcy wished, in the name of all that was decent, that the mention of it did not instantly bring to mind every vision he had ever had to that effect—of holding her, of brushing the hair from her forehead as she did so often herself, of waking her with a kiss—of loving her. He clenched a fist beneath the table, forcing his mind clear of hopes to which he had forfeited any right.

Naturally. I meant, why did you conceal it from me?

"Well, though you were only *half* dead, you were scarcely well enough to have slept in there, even after you began to improve. You would only have felt guilty had you known."

When were you planning on telling me?

"Never, if I could help it."

Never. The word cut Darcy to the quick. She never intended to see him again once they were away from this place.

"I have been humiliated enough," she said sharply. "Quite apart from the obvious indignities we have endured this week, you also think my relations are inferior, my sisters and mother are ridiculous, and that I am some sort of impertinent, headstrong creature who walks alone about the countryside for the simple pleasure of troubling as many people as may be, against every reasonable objection. It is plain from the way you have glowered at my unwashed hair and ill-fitting dress all week what your real opinion of me is. So yes, I was very happy for you to believe I was being at least a *little* ladylike beyond that door."

"*No, no, no, no, no!*" Darcy eschewed the insipid gesture of an extended a finger and firmly shook his head, determined that she should know how wrong she was regardless of what it cost him, but she began speaking again.

"What a waste of time! After all your warnings against impropriety and credulity, I wandered with wilful ignorance directly into Mr Latimer's path and proved your every reproof of me true. Had I been blind, I could not have been more wretchedly imperceptive. You were right—this is a truly unkind world."

To Darcy's utter mortification, she burst into tears. He observed her in wretched suspense, wanting nothing more than to take her into his arms, yet painfully aware he could not. Eventually, when he could watch her distress no longer, he went so far as to reach and very gently squeeze her hand to gain her attention.

"*I wish I were not right. I wish it were not that sort of world.*" His lips were too heavy to form words clearly; Elizabeth frowned at his mouth. He picked up the pen and concluded,

But it is. I know, because of what my own childhood friend did to my sister.

Her face fell. "Mr Wickham?"

He made the gesture for yes. She closed her eyes and looked pained, cementing his opinion of what her feelings for Wickham must be. Seeing it hurt even more than he expected. Hurt so much, it took his breath away. The pain spread like fire around his neck. The room abruptly shrank to a pinpoint before his eyes, and he dropped the pen to grip the edge of the table.

"What is the matter? Are you—oh no! You are bleeding again!"

"Oh," he thought indistinctly. "Not Wickham's fault then." That made a change.

"What have you done?" Elizabeth said urgently, closer by than she had been a moment ago and fussing at his bandages. "Does it pain you?"

Darcy hardly knew. His neck had not hurt as much for a while now. Or, perhaps it was only that everything else had begun to hurt more. He blinked his vision clear, fumbled for the pen, and wrote,

I must tell you—

"No!" she interrupted. "You can tell me whatever it is when you are better."

I comprehend that you do not wish to hear ill of him, but—

"It is not that! Look at you—you can barely sit in that chair! You must rest."

That would not do. He had no confidence whatsoever that if he closed his eyes now, he would ever wake again, and then who would warn her? He fixed his eyes on her. "*Please.*"

She let out a long, silent breath and sat back in her chair, regarding him warily. "Very well."

Good. Now he had only to find the words—and write them, with a hand that could scarcely hold a pen.

My father was Wickham's godfather. Supported him at school and Cambridge.
Highest opinion of him. Favourite.

He tried to dip the pen in the ink but hit it on the side of the well and knocked it out of his grasp. It rolled across the table and fell onto the floor. He watched it, too absorbed with the effort of composing a coherent report to be able to think what to do about a lost pen. He continued to look as Elizabeth bent to retrieve it, dipped it in the ink, and placed it back in his hand, curling his fingers around it.

"Go on," she said softly. "I am listening."

Dear God, he loved her. If leaving this place meant never seeing her again, he wished the damned snow would never melt. Let it be winter forever.

"Sir?"

With an effort, he refocused his gaze. With an even greater effort, he recalled himself to his task.

My father hoped Wickham would go into the church. Recommended to me in
his will that I provide for him in it, plus legacy of £1,000. Wickham resolved
against taking orders. Took £3,000 in lieu of preferment & resigned all claim to
assistance in the church.

Elizabeth took the pen from his hand. He looked up, bewildered.

"You have run out of ink," she said, dipping it in the well and handing it back to him. Darcy looked at the page. The last part of what he had written was mere scratches upon the paper. He rubbed his eyes with the back of his hand and pressed on, tracing over the missing words and continuing with the next.

> *Heard little of him for about 3 yrs until living fell vacant once more & he applied to me again for the presentation, which I refused.*

He glanced up, willing Elizabeth to be convinced of the truth in what he was about to write. He needed to convince her of this, above all, for her own good.

> *Wickham is not the sort of man who ought to be a clergyman. My father never saw his vicious propensities or want of principle. Nor his idleness & dissipation.*

He paused again, waited for her to look at him, then mouthed clearly and emphatically, "*I saw.*"

Elizabeth made no response. Did she believe him? From her expression, he could tell only that she was troubled, not whether by Wickham's actions or his own. He pressed on. If there were one event likely to persuade her to take care, it was the most recent.

> *Did not see him again until last summer. My sister, then 15, was in Ramsgate with her companion. Thither also went Wickham.*

He dipped the pen, then stared at the page until the words ceased jumping about before he could see where to begin the next line.

> *By various means, which I presently have not the strength to narrate, he so far recommended himself to Georgiana that she believed herself in love & consented to an elopement.*

Darcy had no idea whether Elizabeth's small gasp meant she believed him or thought him a wicked liar. He regretted the haste with which he whipped his head up to try and catch her expression, for it did something horrible to his throat and made him cough. Pain sent his thoughts scattering, and it was all he could do to keep to his chair. One of the candles guttered and fizzed with his every panting breath, and he stared at it for want of anything else to anchor him to the world.

"Can I do anything?" Elizabeth enquired softly. "Shall I fetch you a drink?"

The candle's aura expanded and popped, and the room fell back into focus. Darcy shifted his gaze to Elizabeth but could neither recall what she had asked nor think what he had been about to say. He looked down. The word *elopement* loomed large on the page, recalling him mercilessly to Wickham's misdeeds, from which it seemed even near-death would give him no reprieve. Mechanically, he picked up the pen and endeavoured to finish his tale.

> *Chief object unquestionably my sister's fortune of £30,000. Though revenge likely a strong inducement.*

"Was he successful?" Elizabeth asked.

"*No, thank God. I arrived in time to prevent it.*" He forgot to look at her as he mouthed this, and she was obliged to lean around him to read his lips. The pitiless candle put its shadows on all those parts of her face as would plague him the most with the emphasis of her beauty. Looking at her was bittersweet torture. "*I was looking for you.*"

"Pardon?"

"*The day of the accident. I rode through Meryton in the hope of seeing you.*"

Elizabeth sat back, seemingly unsure how to respond. Perchance she had not understood him. He would have written it down, but he could no longer feel his fingers. "*I do not stare at you because your hair is unwashed. I stare because you have utterly bewitched me.*"

"Darcy, I think you must have a fever. Let me fetch some snow to cool you—"

"*I am not feverish. I have felt this way for many months. Long before I left Hert-fordshire.*" He was beset with sudden anxiety and reached for her hand. "*I must warn you about Wickham.*"

"You already have. Look."

He could not fathom why she pointed at a pile of papers on the table. "*No, I must tell you. I would not see you ill-used.*"

"I shall not be, not now. I thank you. I comprehend the mortification you must have felt in revealing this to me."

He screwed up his face, attempting to untangle her words. Mortified? Indeed, she looked to be, though he could not comprehend why. Mayhap she regretted refusing his offer of dancing a reel. Perhaps she would agree if he asked again. He stood up, then could not recall for what purpose. It did not signify, for he did not remain standing for long. He stared at the ceiling and wondered who was weeping.

"Can you hear me? Oh, what has happened? I do not understand why you are so ill!" Something warm came to rest upon his chest. Something that begged him, "Please do not die! I am sorry! I am sorry I ever believed him. I am sorry I said all those awful things. Darcy, please, *please* do not die."

As well as the weeping, and the ringing in his ears, the bear was back, hammering at the door again with fierce insistence.

"Darcy? Darcy, are you in there? Open up, 'tis I, Fitzwilliam!"

That was odd. That was all, too, for darkness closed its maw and smoth-ered everything in oblivion.

Every Way Horrible

The world made itself known by increments. The indistinct rumble of male voices. Light, silhouetting blurred shapes. Soft warmth beneath him, terrible thirst within. A desolate ache in the vicinity of his heart. Darcy's first conscious thought was of Elizabeth, and that he had lost her.

"About time, man. I have grown decidedly weary of watching you grow a beard in your sleep."

Darcy blinked until the smudge of colour looming over him materialised into his cousin Fitzwilliam.

"Is he awake?" Another face appeared above him. Ladbroke? It must be serious if his eldest cousin had bestirred himself to keep vigil also.

"His eyes are open," Fitzwilliam replied. "But I am not convinced he is *compos mentis*. Darcy, can you hear us?"

"Of course I can. You are shouting in my face."

Both brothers frowned and in unison stood away from the bed. "He is still unable to speak."

"Hmm. Farnham, what make you of this?"

"If you would allow me to examine the patient—"

"Perhaps he just needs a drink. Morby? Fetch some wine, there's a fellow."

"If I may, my lord, perhaps boiled water would be more advisable."

Darcy closed his eyes again. Being an invalid had been far more enjoyable when there had been but one much calmer, far sweeter, and eminently prettier person attending him. Where was she at present? His last memory was of the harrowed expression in her eyes as he divulged the truth about Wickham. The need to know what had transpired since then was suffocating. He opened his eyes and fixed them on the nearest person—his manservant. Good. He held up a hand and indicated with the inward curl of his fingers that he required assistance. Morby, ever astute, gave his arm directly, and with gritted teeth, Darcy gripped it and hauled himself to sit upright.

"Hell's bells, what are you doing, man?"

"That is unwise, Mr Morby. Mr Darcy ought not to be upright."

"Darcy, for God's sake, lie back down!"

When the room ceased spinning, Darcy exchanged a knowing look with his man then indicated with a glance the carafe on the nightstand. He held up a hand to forestall his cousins' continued remonstrations and the austere edicts of the man he now recognised as the family's physician, Mr Farnham. He would be able to answer none of their questions until he had quenched his unbearable thirst.

It was not until he had drunk more than half of what Morby poured for him that it occurred to Darcy with what ease he had swallowed it. He lowered the glass to his lap and took a cautious but deep breath—and suffered not the slightest discomfort. He braced himself for pain and deliberately coughed. It made an odd sound, not one readily recognisable as a cough, but it hurt less than expected. He raised a hand to his throat. It was bandaged still, and a careful attempt to move his head from side to side was quickly curtailed by the discovery that it was yet exceedingly tender. Less than it had been, though.

A ripple of anticipation passed through him at the prospect of being recovered enough to speak. He turned to Fitzwilliam and said the first thing that came to mind. "Where is Elizabeth?"

Blast it! He did not choke on it, as he had done on every other utterance since the accident, but neither did he produce anything even closely resembling speech, only a whispery sort of exhalation.

"What was that?" Fitzwilliam replied. "Can you say it more slowly?"

Darcy sighed. *Back to this then*, he thought ruefully. He finished the remainder of his drink, handed the glass to Morby, and signalled for a pen and paper. Whilst that was being found, he submitted to, and apparently passed, a cursory examination by Farnham.

"Your pulse and temperature are perfectly regular, Mr Darcy. And your pallor has improved significantly over the last few days."

"*Few days?*" He had some hazy recollections, now that it was mentioned—of these walls, and this bed, and other people who were not Elizabeth fussing around him with spoons of this and ladles of that. None of it struck him with any peculiar clarity, however.

"You have been up to your nose hairs with laudanum since Monday evening," Ladbroke informed him from where he stood regarding proceedings from the window. "Today is Thursday."

"*Fever?*" Darcy guessed.

"Nay, sir," Farnham answered. "You were exceedingly fortunate in that regard. Your wound took no infection at all."

"*What then?*"

"Farnham here thinks you were just hungry," Fitzwilliam said with evident glee.

"Oh, ah, in addition to a probable concussion," the physician himself added hastily. "And undernourishment is not to be taken lightly. I understand your injury meant that you ate and drank but little the whole time you were in that place, Mr Darcy. Any significant wound takes a vast toll on the body. One requires sustenance to recover. Excessive thirst in particular can cause severe disorientation such as your...*acquaintance* described."

They had spoken to Elizabeth then!

"I have stitched the wound itself now," he went on. "It ought to be more comfortable now that it has had a chance to begin healing."

Darcy made his customary gesture for yes, but it only provoked them all to peer quizzically at his hands. "*It is,*" he mouthed instead. "*And my voice?*" He pointed to his throat to assist Farnham in understanding.

The physician grimaced. "I am afraid I cannot say with any certainty when or whether it will return, sir, but it is not a hopeless case. It was necessary only for me to stitch the soft tissue. Your oesophagus and trachea were intact—severely bruised, hence your difficulty breathing and swallowing—but intact. It would not be unreasonable to hope that once the surrounding contusion heals, your vocal cords will likewise recover."

This was welcome news indeed. "*No other damage?*" he enquired, for after a week of the most disagreeable ignorance, he would know every detail possible.

"It does not appear so, sir," Farnham replied. He began gesturing with his hands as he warmed to his topic. "The musculature of the neck is tremendously thick, designed to protect all the critical structures inside. The mechanism of your injury—a blunt force to this area, here—appears to have ruptured the skin without directly compromising any of those deeper structures."

"*Miss Bennet said I bled profusely.*"

Farnham clearly did not understand, but after two more attempts, Fitzwilliam managed to translate for him.

"It was a large gash," Farnham replied. "There would still have been significant bleeding, but I assure you no major blood vessels were damaged. You would not have survived an injury of that nature."

"I daresay it was still more blood than Miss Bennet is ever likely to have seen," Fitzwilliam said.

"I should think it was a good deal more *man* than she is ever likely to have seen either," Ladbroke added with a lascivious grin.

Darcy pretended to ignore him, but his cousin was not the first to whom that thought had occurred. It had been impossible, whilst submitting to Elizabeth's ministrations, not to wonder what she thought of his exposed person.

Reflecting on her opinion of his appearance only reminded him what he now knew to be her opinion of his character, exacerbating the hollow sensation presently residing just below his ribcage. Nevertheless, the need to discover how she fared lent his actions a fervent quality when Morby returned with writing apparatus. He wasted no time in snatching the pen and paper from his man before inching along the bed closer to the nightstand and leaning upon it to write,

Where is Miss Bennet? And is she well?

He held it up. Fitzwilliam read it, widened his eyes expressively, and, with the flat of his hand, firmly pushed Darcy's arm downwards until the paper lay face down on the bed. "Thank you, Farnham. That will be all for now."

"Very good, Colonel." The physician gathered up his belongings and left.

"We will ring the bell if you are needed again, Morby," Ladbroke said to Darcy's man, who waited for a look of permission from his master before following the physician from the room.

"Good God, Darcy, are you still riding high?" Fitzwilliam exclaimed as soon as the door clicked closed. "You have barely escaped this mess unshackled as it is. Show a little discretion, would you?"

Darcy stared at him in consternation for one or two seconds before whipping the sheet of paper back into the air and jabbing it angrily with his finger. *"Answer my bloody question!"*

"Very well," his cousin answered warily. "She is returned to her family. And, at the last I heard, in perfect health."

Darcy could not smile. That she was well was a vast relief. That she was gone back to her family, and away from him possibly forever, made him wretched. *"And when did you last hear?"*

"Pardon?"

He bared his teeth, slapped the paper back on the nightstand, and scribbled upon it,

Has there been no further word since Monday?

Fitzwilliam came to lean over him and read aloud what he had written, for Ladbroke's benefit. There was a pause afterwards. Darcy wished they would cease looking at each other in that irritating way, as though privately communicating how they ought to manage him into compliance. He added a line to his note.

"'I have lost my voice, not my wits,'" Fitzwilliam read, quickly adding, "That is heartening to know, Darcy. Nevertheless, you do seem uncommonly concerned about the young lady."

"Perchance more happened at the inn than we have been informed," Ladbroke remarked.

"*What do you take me for?*" Darcy mouthed angrily.

His cousin wasted very little time attempting to comprehend him before giving up with a shake of his head. "I can see you are angry, but you must agree it is singularly out of character for you to show such a marked interest in a girl of her calibre."

The truth of it shamed Darcy deeply and made him more determined to prove Elizabeth's true worth.

She did much to aid my recovery.

A wholly inadequate explanation on paper that felt even more deficient when Fitzwilliam read it aloud with perfect indifference.

"We comprehend she was very good to you," Ladbroke replied. "But, you know, it would not do to appear over grateful."

"*Meaning?*"

"You are aware, I presume, that the relatives with whom she is staying live near Cheapside. Watling Street is the direction she gave when we sent for her uncle to fetch her. Seriously, Darcy. *Watling Street.*" He scoffed contemptuously. "You must take care to give them no reason to think they can expect anything from you. Give these people an inch, and they will take a yard."

Darcy winced. This, then, was how he had sounded to Elizabeth. With this same unfounded and despicable contempt had he paraded his prepossessions before her.

What, other than their residing in the City, makes you suppose they expect anything from me?

"That alone would be enough to rouse my suspicions. But if it is proof you desire, the uncle has already come sniffing around once."

"*What?*" Darcy scrabbled to replenish the ink on the pen.

He has called here? For what purpose?

Ladbroke deferred, with a look, to Fitzwilliam, who answered, "He claimed to have come on behalf of his niece to enquire after your well-being."

Hope exploded in Darcy's chest, dislodging a nebulous memory that bubbled to the surface of his laudanum-addled mind and popped into coherence: "Darcy, please do not die." People who cared whether one lived or died were surely beyond enmity. His other memory—of Elizabeth's dismay at hearing Wickham traduced—abruptly blurred and transformed into something that might just as easily be construed as concern for *him*. Perchance he had not lost her after all.

It did not occur to you that her interest might have been genuine?

"It would not matter if she were in complete earnest," Ladbroke objected. "They are of absolutely no consideration in the world, Darcy."

She is a gentleman's daughter.

"Aye. A gentleman of paltry income whose estate is entailed upon Lady Catherine's parson, we are reliably informed."
"By whom?"
"Lady Catherine, of course. You know how she likes to be an authority on every subject. Her new incumbent is cousin to Miss Bennet, apparently. Once she discovered she knew the identity of your saviour, she was most forthcoming on the matter. That is all by the by, though. The material point is that unless you wish to saddle yourself with the most inferior connexions in Christendom, you must not encourage them."

I care nothing for her connexions. I owe her —

But Fitzwilliam was leaning over him, reading his words as he put them on the page, and before he could write *my life,* Ladbroke interrupted.
"Yes, yes. We have attempted to reimburse the family, but they have resisted. My guess is that they hope, by refusing immediate recompense, to secure a more lasting reward."
"What do you mean, you have attempted to reimburse them?"
Ladbroke screwed up his face. "Eh?"
Darcy shoved the pen in the ink and almost broke the nib scratching out,

What do you mean!

"Calm yourself," Fitzwilliam said. "You have only just awoken. You must not overexert yourself."
"What do you think I mean? We are not brutes," Ladbroke said, ignoring his brother. "You bled all over her clothes, apparently, so my mother offered her a sum of money to replace them." He waved a hand insouciantly in the air. "Plus a token amount in recognition of her assistance. Enough to dissuade them from embroiling you in any scandal—or so we hoped."
After a moment of disbelief, Darcy threw the pen down in despair and pinched the bridge of his nose. Elizabeth cared enough to have sent her uncle to ask after him, and his family had attempted to buy the man off and then sent him on his way. The cruel irony of him ever having disdained *her* relations made a mockery of everything.
"Perhaps you had better go," he heard Fitzwilliam say quietly. Darcy could almost hear Ladbroke roll his eyes in response, though his cousin's parting words were more generous.
"I shall see you in a while, Darcy. It is very good to have you back with us."

Fitzwilliam saw Ladbroke to the door and on his return, dragged a chair with him, in which he sat, crossed his arms, and leant back until the front legs lifted off the floor. "What is all this about then?" he enquired. "You seem more concerned about this Miss Bennet than you do about the very real prospect of being imposed upon in some way. I comprehend that she assisted you, but that does not oblige you to be shackled to her forevermore."

"Your concerns about Miss Bennet are wholly without founda—"

"I am afraid I shall have to stop you there," Fitzwilliam interrupted. He stood, caught and righted his chair as it toppled from the only two legs in use, and returned to the nightstand to point at the inkwell. "You are going to have to write it down."

Darcy gritted his teeth. He sincerely hoped his voice was not permanently gone, for the struggle of making himself understood was becoming intolerably vexatious.

> *None of you need concern yourselves about Miss Bennet. She is not mercenary, else she would not have turned down an offer from her cousin—heir to Longbourn. It would have secured her future and that of her whole family, yet she refused him because she did not respect him.*

It observably gave Fitzwilliam pause, but not so much that he ceased his objections completely. "Or perhaps she turned him down because she had set her sights higher."

> *Give it up, Fitzwilliam. She has no wish to marry me.*

That earned him a piercing look. "You seem very certain of that."

> *I am even more certain of it now that Lady Matlock has attempted to bribe her into silence.*

"My mother had only your best interests in mind. It did not occur to any of us that you might actually have designs on the young lady."

> *I have known Miss Bennet for many months, not just this one week.*

"Yes, she told me you met in Hertfordshire last year. She did not elaborate on the nature of your acquaintance, though—which, it would appear, was closer than any of us supposed."

Darcy avoided answering directly and wrote,

> *Her integrity is one of many reasons you need not worry for my reputation.*

He took his time replenishing the ink and held his hand over the page for a long moment before adding,

My reputation is not the only one she is protecting. She knows about Wickham and Georgiana.

"What? How?"

It is a long story, but you must not be anxious. I trust her implicitly.

Fitzwilliam looked at him long and hard—a look that Darcy met unflinchingly until his cousin let out a harsh sigh and stalked away across the room. "We must hope your trust is well placed."

It is better placed than your mother's suspicions. Her good intentions notwithstanding, this attempt to buy Miss Bennet's secrecy, when she was already concealing so much on my behalf, is an insult I can scarcely think on without abhorrence.

Darcy held the note out until Fitzwilliam came back and snatched it from him. He did not speak immediately after reading it, but leant against the window, looking out as he ruminated on it.

"I grant you," he said at length, "if she was intent on blackmail, Georgiana's misadventure must present a far greater likelihood of success than the rumour of a few days at an unknown inn with a man as far beyond her reach as you. She has given no indication that she means to reveal any of it."

Darcy fixed his cousin with an unyielding look. "*She will not.*"

"Well, I am convinced *you* believe it at least."

Darcy nodded once in acknowledgement—and mouthed an oath at the pain it induced, which seemed all the worse after not having felt it for so long.

"Better?" Fitzwilliam enquired, once he had regained his composure. Darcy almost laughed that he should ask another question requiring a nod in response. He had forgotten how well Elizabeth had learnt to evade such questions. He eschewed answering at all and wrote another note instead,

How was she? When you found us?

He held it up. Fitzwilliam walked closer to peer at it, then frowned deeply. "She was distraught—which I attributed at first to her being frightened by your being comatose and bleeding on the floor. I have wondered since whether she formed an attachment to you in the course of your time together, but that seems unlikely if what you say is true."

Darcy had thought the same at one time. After she had grown flustered watching his lips; whilst she had held his hand as he spoke about his mother. It all seemed moot now, for since then, they had stood in the snow, arguing bitterly about his selfishness, and his family had insulted her in the worst way imaginable. Nevertheless, he could not easily dismiss the tiny ray of hope he felt in knowing that, of all the horrors Elizabeth had endured last week, none had rendered her distraught—only his malaise, apparently.

"But you do admire her?" Fitzwilliam enquired.

"*I do.*" He fancied his cousin comprehended his sincerity as, for once, he did not ridicule him.

Taught to Hope

There was nothing more to be said on the matter that was not either awkward or painful and thus, when a knock on the door interrupted the exchange, neither man was disappointed. Fitzwilliam looked at it expectantly. Darcy looked at Fitzwilliam and waited for him to notice, raising an eyebrow when he eventually turned a puzzled expression his way.

"Oh, yes! Forgive me, I quite forgot!" On Darcy's behalf, Fitzwilliam barked, "Come!"

The door inched open and around it peered such a heartwarming sight as cheered Darcy considerably. "*Georgiana!*"

His sister opened the door fully and came in, though his muteness evidently disturbed her, for she cast an anxious glance at Fitzwilliam rather than reply to him.

"It is well, Georgiana," her cousin assured her. "Your brother has not yet recovered his voice, but he is much improved."

Darcy held out his arm and gestured for her to come to him, which she did, whilst simultaneously beginning to weep. He put one arm about her and cradled her head against his shoulder. With his free hand, he scooped up his notes from his nightstand and held them out for Fitzwilliam to dispose of. There was no need for Georgiana to learn that her misadventures had been disclosed to anyone.

"We were so worried!" his sister sobbed. "Morby told us you were not an hour behind him when he set out."

"This is true, he did," Fitzwilliam said with a cynical tone. "And had you stayed on the Great North Road, you would have had no trouble, for they had men working to keep it clear for the stagecoaches all week. You gave us a rum chase searching for you in every ditch between here and Cooper's Corner. We never thought to look for you along Ermine Street. Indeed, there was no plausible reason for you to go that way."

Darcy grimaced apologetically at his cousin, then gently moved his sister away from his shoulder and mouthed an apology to her. She squinted at his lips, and he did his best to conceal his exasperation that even such a simple phrase should be incomprehensible. "*Sorry,*" he tried again.

"Oh, you do not need to apologise. I am only relieved you are home and well. You cannot imagine our relief when we received your letter. Though it was tempered by Miss Bennet's account of your condition."

He frowned at her in query and, when she did not take his cue, at his cousin.

"Miss Bennet added her own note to yours," Fitzwilliam explained. "She felt you had not done justice to the severity of your injury and urged us to do all we could to reach you with haste."

Darcy smiled, recalling wistfully Elizabeth's teasing while they composed his letter together and loving her all the more for not concerning him with her clandestine plea for urgency. "*And still you mistrusted her?*" he mouthed.

Fitzwilliam peered closely at him, muttering, "Still… mistrust…still I mistrusted her? Of course! More so, after that, for you would be no good to a self-seeker dead, would you!"

Georgiana gasped loudly. "Miss Bennet would take advantage of you? That cannot be!"

Darcy snarled in vexation at his cousin and twisted to the nightstand to dash off a few lines on a new sheet of paper.

> *Miss Bennet absolutely did <u>not</u> attempt to exploit me.*

To ease Georgiana's mind, and in no way to exculpate anybody else, he added,

> *It is only that none of our family was acquainted with her. Prudence demanded that they were wary.*

He passed the note to his sister.

"They ought to have asked me," she said upon reading it. "I could have told them of the favourable reports you gave her in your letters to me from Netherfield last autumn. It is the same Miss Bennet, is it not? It was quite near her home in Hertfordshire that the accident happened."

Darcy pretended not to notice the way Fitzwilliam was looking at him, and mouthed, "*Yes, somewhere near there.*"

"And she was so kind to me. I could never believe she would take advantage of anybody."

The incongruity of such a remark did not go unnoticed by either gentleman, and while Fitzwilliam frowned over it, Darcy wrote,

When has Miss Bennet had the opportunity to be kind to you?

"The night you were brought home. You looked so very ill, I thought you must be about to die, but everybody was running about, shouting, and I had no idea what was happening. I do not blame anybody for attending to you—I should have been dismayed had they not, only I was very frightened. And Miss Bennet comforted me."

"*She is very caring,*" he mouthed. "*I am glad you liked her.*"

Georgiana shook her head, obviously unable to understand him, and continued as though he had not spoken. "She assured me that you were not going to die."

"That was brash," Fitzwilliam remarked. "Even I would not have given you that assurance on Monday evening. None of us were convinced it was the case."

"Oh, but she was only making a joke."

Darcy joined his cousin in looking askance at Georgiana. She blushed deeply, which scarcely surprised him, for his sister had none of the same courage to be impertinent as Elizabeth.

"*What did she say?*" he mouthed. Only when Fitzwilliam repeated the question aloud did his sister explain.

"Well, she said…pardon me…she said that you like to have your own way rather too well, but that in this case it would prove invaluable, for it was very unlikely that you wished to die, therefore she could not see that you would allow it to happen."

Fitzwilliam snorted with laughter. "I like her better by the moment."

So did Darcy.

"She *was* only joking, though," Georgiana stammered. "I have made it seem as though she spoke unkindly of you, but that is not true. She spoke very highly of how brave you had been."

Darcy restrained his response to a raised eyebrow, though his heart leapt like a boy's at the unexpected praise.

"She said you never complained, despite being in a great deal of pain with no means of relieving it, and that you were concerned for her safety and comfort above your own throughout."

These words were of greater comfort to Darcy than any pain relief, further swelling his burgeoning hope. He knew enough of Elizabeth's disposition to be certain that, had she still been convinced he was a selfish and conceited being, she would never have mollified Georgiana with false platitudes such as these. Though he comprehended that it made him appear somewhat ridiculous, he could not resist appealing for more particulars.

Did she say anything else?

"Not that I recall. Her uncle arrived shortly after that to take her away. She did beg me to keep her informed as to your recovery, but it is not a promise I have been able to keep, for nobody knows where her uncle lives."

Darcy turned to glare at Fitzwilliam.

He splayed his hands and gave a barely contrite shrug. "Prudence demanded we were wary."

"I wish I could have sent word," Georgiana said, "for notwithstanding all her attempts to assure me, it was obvious that she was very worried about you. And what with Lady Catherine being uncivil to her, I should imagine she was—"

Darcy interrupted her with a hand on her arm. "*Lady Catherine was here?*"

"Pardon?"

He grabbed the paper and impatiently echoed what he had said in a note.

"Everybody was here," his sister replied.

"Lady Catherine travelled to London as soon as she heard you were missing," Fitzwilliam informed him. "She has been staying with my mother and father, which has made them twice as anxious as the rest of us to see you expeditiously recovered."

Darcy ignored him. There was but one person for whose inconvenience at the hands of Lady Catherine he cared.

In what way was she uncivil to Miss Bennet?

Georgiana leant over to read this and then sat up and began wringing her hands. "It was a bit of a misunderstanding, I think. When Miss Bennet's uncle arrived to collect her, he was quite cross that she had been left to sit in the entrance hall. If he had seen your condition when you arrived moments before, and the commotion in the house, I am sure he would not have been so angry. I certainly did not sit with her there with any design to be insulting; it was just where we ended up after you were taken upstairs.

"I imagine, though, that he has been as worried about his niece as we all were about you, and...well, I can comprehend why he was vexed at the apparent slight. I know you would have been, had it been me. Only Lady Catherine did not take kindly to his manner of speaking to the footman when he expressed his displeasure. I was sent upstairs, and I believe they left directly, but from what I heard, my aunt was not very gracious in her farewell."

Darcy said nothing. He could scarcely bear to consider the disregard with which his family had treated the woman who saved his life and dared not suppose what effect their behaviour might have had on his already tenuous chances of securing Elizabeth's affections.

"Darcy, I am heartily sorry that happened," Fitzwilliam said with more earnestness than any of his previous excuses. "I knew nothing of it until this moment. I would never have been so uncivil—"

He stopped when Darcy thrust a hastily scrawled note at him.

No, you waited until his next call and then insulted him with the offer of hush money!

Could any more possibly have been done to ensure Elizabeth would never love him? He had to apologise. If she never spoke to him again afterwards, he would have to accept the loss, but he could not rest until she knew how sorry he was. He tossed the pen down and stood up only for the lightheadedness of his last day at the inn to return with a vengeance.

Fitzwilliam lunged forward to lend his support, demanding, "What are you doing?" as he propped him up by the elbow.

"*I mean to call on Elizabeth.*"

"Say that again?"

"*There is no need to shout. I am mute, not deaf.*"

"Stop babbling, man, I cannot understand you!"

Darcy elbowed him off and leant over the nightstand to write a note.

I must apologise to Miss Bennet.

He left it where it was for his cousin to read and took a few unsteady steps to pull the bell for Morby.

"Do not be ridiculous," Fitzwilliam said behind him. "You are in no state to go anywhere. Get back into bed."

Darcy ignored him and walked to the dresser to splash water on his face.

"I comprehend that you feel responsible, but another day will make little difference. Go tomorrow, or the next day—whenever you have regained strength enough to walk across a room without stumbling into things."

"He is right, Brother," Georgiana added. "You really are not well enough to go."

They *were* right, of course, but Darcy did not mean to choose this moment to disappoint Elizabeth by failing to get his way, and when Morby arrived into the room, he pointed at himself and mouthed, "*Dress me.*"

To his consternation, and for the first time in the man's employ, Morby looked first to someone else for corroboration of his instructions, his alarm evident.

"See, Darcy?" Fitzwilliam said. "You are convincing no one with this behaviour that you are in your right mind. Stand down, Morby. The stubborn ox is going nowhere."

Darcy reviled the weakness in his knees that prevented him walking to the closet himself to pull out some clothes. He drew several deep breaths and was rallying himself to give a convincing show of strength when there came another knock at the door, and the answer to a good number of his problems bounded into the room.

"Upon my life, Darcy, you look awful! What the devil are you doing out of bed?"

"Bingley, thank God! I need your help."

"ARE YOU SURE YOU ARE WELL ENOUGH TO BE SITTING UP? I AM CERTAIN YOU could still manage to write me notes if you were propped up in bed."

I have been lying down for the better part of a fortnight. Humour me.

Darcy had got rid of his sister and cousin only on the promise of returning to his bed to rest, but he had several pressing matters to attend to before he did that. Despite them having appraised Bingley of all the details of his ordeal and rescue before they left, he had a fair amount yet to relay to his friend. Sitting up would make the task far easier, thus he had settled himself at his small breakfast table.

"Very well." Bingley gave up hovering over him and slid into the opposite seat.

Darcy indicated with the pen for him to move the chair nearer. *"So you can read what I write."*

"What?"

Darcy refrained from allowing his lips to move with the oath he said to himself. These things had all been elementary to Elizabeth. Why could nobody else fathom them without detailed instruction?

It will save me turning the paper towards you each time I want you to read what I have written. Should save a good hour of our lives.

With pantomime exaggeration, he turned the paper and pushed it across the table for Bingley to read.

"Ah, right you are." His friend obligingly shuffled his chair around the table. That much closer, he was distracted with peering at Darcy's bandages. "You cannot have been kicked with full force, can you? It would have killed you."

"It nearly did." He did not even wait to see whether Bingley had comprehended and switched immediately to writing instead.

But yes, it can only have been a glancing blow. Fortunately for me.

"Indeed. I am very sorry for you, Darcy. It is a ghastly thing to have happened. We were all frightfully worried about you when we heard. Caroline has been beside herself."

Darcy dipped his head to conceal a smile at the recollection of his many conversations with Elizabeth about that lady. His injury prevented him from dipping very far, however, and he was caught out.

"Now look here," Bingley said, laughing, "my sister might be overly effusive in her praise, but she has a very genuine affection for you. And your house."

His muttered addendum made Darcy laugh outright—which came out as more of a crackling wheeze that startled Bingley out of all humour.

"Good God, what is the matter? Shall I fetch somebody?"

Darcy held up a hand to allay his friend's fears and could not help but think that if this slight rasp was cause for such alarm, it was an exceedingly good job he had not been in Bingley's care earlier in the week, when he had sounded as though he was leaking air from every inch of his windpipe. He pointed with the pen at the paper. *"Shall we begin?"*

Bingley nodded, and so he began.

> *I have two things to tell you, and a favour to ask of you. I will keep this very simple. The first is that I am in love with Miss Elizabeth Bennet.*

Reading this once apparently did not suffice, and after his first perusal, Bingley swooped down until his nose almost touched the page to read it a second time. Then he reared up again and turned to stare at Darcy incredulously. "In *love?* With Miss *Elizabeth?*"

Darcy indicated the page with a glance.

"Oh yes," Bingley said, leaning back out of the way of the paper and ink, though not without continuing to send astonished glances in Darcy's direction.

> *I formed an attachment at Netherfield but was fool enough to think I should— and could—overcome it. My affections have grown beyond all wish to repress them during our time together this week.*

"I see," Bingley said stiffly.

> *Her feelings for me are far less certain, however.*

"Are they, indeed? What a coincidence."

Darcy could easily discern his friend was not happy, and rightly so, but he could only explain one thing at a time. He would get to the part Bingley would like better after this.

> *I have not behaved as well as I ought to have over the course of our*

acquaintance. *More to the point, since returning to London, my family have treated her infamously. My wishes aside, I would at least have her know that I am sorry.*

"Very noble, I am sure."

The favour I would ask of you is this: will you call on her, today if possible, and deliver that apology for me? I cannot countenance a delay of another four-and-twenty hours or more.

Bingley pursed his lips and frowned at the question on the page. "You wish me to call on the Bennets' relations?"

I should be very grateful for it, yes.

"Darcy, we have been friends for a long time, and I hope you know there is little I would not do for you. But you must know this is an unreasonable request. After you encouraged me to *forsake* Miss Bennet, I—" He stopped, because Darcy had held up the pen to gain his attention. When Bingley met his eye, Darcy gave him a rueful grin, and when he lowered the pen back to the page, Bingley's eyes followed it thither.

The second thing I wish to tell you—which I probably ought to have told you first—is this: Miss Elizabeth informs me that my assessment of her sister's feelings was incorrect. She assures me that Miss Jane Bennet was, and still is, very much in love with you.

Bingley shoved his chair backwards and sprang to his feet, startling Darcy to such an extent that he jarred his wound painfully.

"Are you certain? Did she—Gads, are you quite well?"

Darcy pried his eyes open and, after a few deep, steadying breaths, unwrapped his fingers from about his throbbing neck. *"I have survived worse."*

Bingley sat back down, his face screwed up with incomprehension. "What was that?"

Darcy sighed resignedly and retrieved the pen.

I am well enough. And I am heartily sorry for having misadvised you. It was very wrong of me to presume to know Miss Bennet's heart better than you. Since there is good reason to believe that she would be receptive to your renewed attentions, however, I am hopeful that whilst officious, my interference may prove not to be ruinous.

Bingley read the note, leant back in his chair with his hands in his pockets, and puffed out his cheeks. "I accept your apology. Other than your partiality for Miss Elizabeth, I comprehended all your other reasoning at the time, which makes me appreciate this present disclosure all the more, for you have evidently rethought more than one part of it."

Darcy could not pretend this revelation did not surprise him, and he admonished himself for underestimating his friend's perceptiveness.

If it is any consolation, I have been thoroughly upbraided by Miss Elizabeth.

"Have you, indeed?" Bingley replied with evident amusement. "I should like to have seen that."

Darcy smiled faintly but refrained from replying. He had received a great many reproofs from Elizabeth—and would gladly endure a good number more, if she would only condescend to see him long enough to deliver them.

"What a day this is turning out to be," Bingley said, more amiably than Darcy deserved. "First you, then Miss Bennet—what am I to have returned to me next, the ten pounds I lost to Clarkson last Saturday?" His pleasure was impossible to mistake. Darcy tried in vain not to envy him the promise of such a felicitous outcome.

I understand Miss Bennet is also at her uncle's house. You would see her there, were you to call with my message for her sister.

Bingley required no further persuasion. With his assurances that he would pass on Darcy's regrets to Elizabeth, as well as his promise to call as soon as he was able, he left, fair skipping out of the house in his eagerness to reignite his courtship with Miss Jane Bennet. Darcy was left to wallow in shame for not having recognised the misery in which he had involved his friend when he separated him from her in the first place. It was just deserts, he supposed, that he should suffer such misery himself, as he waited with very little hope, to discover what Elizabeth's response would be.

Utterly and Completely Speechless

"He should come to Rosings with me. Mr O'Neill would be delighted to oversee his recovery. He was invaluable when Sir Lewis was indisposed."

"I should be far better persuaded by your recommendation had your husband survived his indisposition, Sister. There are plenty more reliable physicians here in Town."

"It is not the physicians to which I object, but the air. The pollution will do his airways no good in his present state. He would do much better nearer the sea."

"I daresay the air at Pemberley would do just as well for him, and he would have his own staff—"

"But at Rosings, Anne could keep him company."

"If Anne were in any way concerned for him, she would be here, not cavorting around Rosings Park in her phaeton."

Darcy closed his eyes and attempted not to hear any of them. His entire family had descended upon the house upon learning of his revival—excepting Anne, which was no great loss. How they all thought their incessant and clamorous bickering was in any way conducive to his recovery, he knew not, but they showed no sign of desisting, despite his every attempt to interject. None of them had the patience to read his lips or await his laboriously written notes. The conversation of so many people flowed too fast for him to keep pace, and though he would not usually tolerate the discourtesy of being ignored, he was presently too tired to object and had given up attempting to make himself understood, or indeed noticed at all, a good half an hour earlier.

He ought probably to have stayed abed, but he could no longer bear the unceasing whir of his thoughts as he envisaged, over and again, Elizabeth's surprise when Bingley arrived at her door. Would she be grateful for news? Would she be unwelcoming? Would she even still be there? Thoughts of it consumed him. He had slept, bathed, shaved, eaten, and slept again, all with limited relief from the torment of suspense, before getting dressed and coming downstairs to seek a more effective distraction. He wished now that he had not, for it had in no way diminished his desperate wish to know all that was being said and felt at one particular address in Watling Street—only now he must endure his relations' quarrelling whilst he waited.

"I think we can all agree that he ought not to remain here."

"If by *all*, you mean *you*, then yes. And by the same token, we may celebrate never disagreeing about anything ever again."

"You have grown too used to yours being the only opinion you ever hear down in Kent, Catherine. I rather think Darcy might have something to say on the matter."

"Darcy is incapable of *saying* anything on *any* matter at present."

"That very obviously does not disqualify him from possessing opinions."

"Aye. You betray a profound misunderstanding of my cousin if you mistake this silence for docility."

Everybody looked in Darcy's direction. He looked back at them all with ill-concealed distaste.

"Well, nephew? What is your wish?"

Assured that nobody would comprehend him, he mouthed, "*That I had asked Miss Bennet for her hand two months ago and done more to earn it, thereby assuring myself of a positive answer and avoiding all this misery.*"

It was almost comical to observe everybody's utter bemusement.

"He cannot possibly stay here if he cannot be understood. How is anybody to know what he is saying?"

"*I am perfectly capable of making myself understood,*" he mouthed, knowing full well this was not the way. "*Whether anybody is willing to take the time to understand me is less certain.*"

"Darcy, you are not even trying, and it is not helping," Fitzwilliam complained.

"You see?" said Lady Catherine. "He is not in his right mind. He is never usually this obdurate."

"Not to you, mayhap," Ladbroke muttered from his spot at the near end of the sofa. "But to everybody else he bally well is."

"Do you not think you ought to go back to bed, Brother?" Georgiana enquired, having crept nearer to him under the cover of the debate. "You look tired."

He smiled at her but did not reply.

"She has a point, Darcy," Ladbroke said.

On Ladbroke's other side sat Fitzwilliam, whither the campaign to banish Darcy back to bed spread like the plague. "Aye, get some rest. You cannot wish to listen to all of us when you are only just out of your stupor."

"What is this? Is he unwell?" demanded Lord Matlock from the armchair at the other end of the sofa. From him, the contagion jumped across the room to his wife.

"Nephew, if you are unwell, you must go to bed. Obstinacy never cured a person of anything."

The spread of dissension completed its circuit of the parlour when it reached Lady Catherine. "Ring the bell, Georgiana. Let somebody come to take him to bed before he collapses."

Darcy indicated to his sister with a small gesture that she was to do no such thing. He was on the verge of evicting them all on the premise of their unanimous opinion that peace and quiet were in his best interests when the door opened, and a footman entered to announce that Bingley had arrived back to see him. Apprehension erupted behind his breastbone, myriad crackling detonations that hastened his pulse and sent his mind reeling in a hundred different directions. He gestured for Bingley to be shown in.

"It is good that you are out of bed, Darcy, for—" His friend stopped in the doorway and looked about the room. "I beg your pardon. I did not realise you had company."

Darcy put both hands out to indicate that it mattered not and mouthed urgently, "*Did you call?*"

"If you just asked whether I called, the answer is yes, I did indeed."

"Are you going to introduce this gentleman, Darcy?" enquired Lady Matlock indignantly.

Darcy clenched his teeth and indicated with a curt gesture to his throat that he could not.

"This is Mr Bingley, Mother. Darcy's friend," Fitzwilliam said for him. Indicating each by turn, he then introduced the rest of the party to Bingley.

"You have met him before, Mother," Ladbroke declared, to which Lady Matlock objected, prompting something of a debate that Fitzwilliam and Lady Catherine wasted no time joining in.

Darcy ignored them all and mouthed a question to Bingley. "*Miss Bennet?*"

"Regrettably, she was not there," he replied beneath the commotion. The sting of Darcy's disappointment was sharp, but lasted only until Bingley added, "She returned to Longbourn before Miss Elizabeth was found, but I have been assured a visit would be welcome. My cause is not lost!"

"*And her sister?*"

A boyish grin overspread Bingley's countenance. "Oh yes, Miss Elizabeth was there."

"*And? Any message?*"

"Well, that is the thing, Darcy. I decided I did not care for being your messenger. I thought it would be easier to cut out the middleman." He stepped further into the room and gestured to somebody beyond the door to come forward. The room fell silent but for the almighty thud of Darcy's heart.

"*Miss Bennet!*" He lurched to his feet then was forced to take hold of the back of the chair to keep from falling over. "*Are you well?*"

Her smile was small, subdued but sublime. "Very well, sir, thank you. You look better."

As did she. Darcy had not appreciated how weary she looked at the inn until he saw her now, rested, bathed, and dressed once more in her own clothes. As one might expect, they showed her to far better advantage than Mrs Stratton's loaned gown. Her hair was handsomely arranged, too, though he missed the way it had used to hang loose about her face.

"Better?" cried Lady Catherine. "Upon my word, Miss Bennet, you cannot be looking properly."

Elizabeth's smile vanished as she took in the array of people filling the parlour, all of whom she had met on Monday evening, but few of whom were presently betraying any greater warmth than they had shown her on that occasion. It amazed Darcy how rapidly his relations, who moments ago had been at each other's throats, could unite in the face of a perceived threat. He rejoiced to observe Elizabeth's courage visibly rise. With no discernible movement, she yet seemed to stand a little straighter, hold her head a little higher, and assume such a look of penetration as might alarm a person unused to it.

The woman with whom she had come appeared considerably less assured and looked uneasily at Bingley.

"Darcy," said his friend with unperturbed ebullience, "allow me to introduce Miss Bennet's aunt, Mrs Gardiner."

To Darcy's dismay, a look of contempt passed amongst his relatives, for despite her appearance as a woman of fashion, they were all well aware from whence Mrs Gardiner had come. Determined to mitigate the slight, he bowed deeply. It was excruciating, but he did his best to ignore the way his stomach knotted in revolt. "*An honour to meet you, madam.*"

Mrs Gardiner looked anxiously at her niece.

"He said it is an honour to meet you," Elizabeth said quietly, sending Darcy a look of gratitude.

"Miss Bennet, it is a pleasure to see you again," Fitzwilliam said, adding his voice to Bingley's attempt to smooth the waters, for which Darcy was inordinately grateful. "I did not have the time on Monday evening to thank you for your kindness towards my cousin. I imagine he does look a good deal better than he did this time last week, for which we are all vastly grateful to you."

Lord Matlock cleared his throat loudly, his eyebrows drawn together in disapprobation. "Let us not deny the physician his due. I am sure Miss Bennet did her best, but we have Farnham to thank for Darcy's recovery."

"Indeed," his wife agreed. "As I told your uncle on Tuesday, Miss Bennet, we are all most obliged for your troubles, but there is no need to concern yourself any further with Mr Darcy's well-being."

Elizabeth smiled noncommittally. Her aunt did not. Darcy could not tell whether Mrs Gardiner were affronted or afraid, but she most certainly was not comfortable.

"*Madam, I beg you would be more civil to my guests,*" he mouthed angrily, but either Lady Matlock did not notice he had addressed her, or she chose to ignore him. He rapped his knuckles on the nearby table until she acknowledged him. "*Farnham only sewed me up. Miss Bennet kept me alive until he could.*"

"What are you saying?" his aunt said crossly.

He rolled his eyes heavenward but persevered, enunciating as clearly as he could. "*I am alive because Miss Bennet kept my wound clean all week.*"

"We cannot understand you, Darcy!" Ladbroke exclaimed, chuckling as though at some inane joke and not his own cousin's misfortune.

"He said that he is alive because he did not contract a fever."

Everybody's attention snapped to Elizabeth.

"And pray," said Lady Catherine coldly, "how is it that you can claim to comprehend him when none of his own family can?"

Comprehend and paraphrase, thought Darcy with amusement.

"After a week of close confinement, your ladyship can hardly be surprised," Elizabeth replied. "Mr Darcy and I have spent considerable time learning to understand one another." She shifted her gaze to his and added, "I comprehend him perfectly now."

Darcy searched her countenance for some indication as to whether that were a good or a bad thing, struggling not to be carried away on a swell of false hope.

"You exaggerate, Miss Bennet," said Lady Matlock. "An entire inn is not such very close confinement."

Lady Catherine narrowed her eyes at Elizabeth. "It would be to nobody's advantage were you to embellish the particulars of the situation, Miss Bennet. Least of all your own."

Darcy knocked on the table again. "*It is no exaggeration, madam. Miss Bennet slept in a cupboard. How confined would you have her be?*"

His aunt frowned furiously at his lips as though she could scare the meaning out of them. "Pardon?"

"If you spoke more slowly, we might stand a chance of understanding you," Fitzwilliam admonished.

"He said it was a small inn," Elizabeth said quietly.

"*Is that what you said?*" Lady Catherine demanded of Darcy.

It was not, yet Elizabeth's plaintive look recalled him to the embarrassment to which she had confessed when *he* discovered the truth of her sleeping arrangements. That he had been about to divulge it to his already scornful relations, even though in her defence, was unforgivable. "*Yes,*" he confirmed, hoping against hope that he had not damaged her opinion of him any further.

Her ladyship's countenance reddened. "Nevertheless, a small inn is still an *entire* inn. There is nothing scandalous to be made of it."

"Miss Bennet has not come here to threaten us with scandal! You just heard Bingley say it was his idea to bring her here!"

Bingley must have caught some of what Darcy mouthed, for he took the cue to defend Elizabeth. "Oh, yes, it was all my idea to bring Miss Bennet for a visit. She was anxious to know that Darcy was better. I suggested that she come with me and see for herself."

Lady Catherine spared Bingley only the briefest glance before she fixed Elizabeth with a disdainful scowl. "Your uncle was too busy in his *shop* to bring you, I suppose."

Good God! Anger made Darcy's heart pound, compounding his lightheadedness. He tightened his grip on the chair back and deliberately slowed his breathing as he struggled to think of a single cogent thing to say in support of Elizabeth, but she started speaking before the ringing in his ears diminished enough to allow coherent thought.

"My uncle was disinclined to come, your ladyship. I understand his previous call was not welcomed." Again, she looked directly at Darcy. "And I know very few men willing to have their honour questioned more than once without any resentment at all. That would require a fineness of character that very few people possess."

Was this meant for him? The wild swing of Darcy's emotions as they veered between despair and hope, anger and elation, exacerbated his struggle to think clearly, and he took too long to acknowledge her. His uncle began opining vociferously and not very politely about the sensibilities of the middle classes, and Elizabeth looked down at the floor, concealing her expression from the room.

"I think we had better go, Lizzy," her aunt said to her quietly.

"No!" Darcy pushed away from the chair to go to her, but it slid sideways an inch and unbalanced him.

"Brother!" exclaimed Georgiana, rushing to his side.

"Darcy, sit down, for God's sake," said Ladbroke on his other.

"Someone send for Mr Farnham."

"I do not need Farnham, I am perfectly well," Darcy mouthed, pushing his sister gently but firmly away from him.

"Pardon?"

"What did you say?"

They all looked at Elizabeth for a translation. She did not give one. Instead she told him, "You had better do as they say, sir. You look very pale."

"I am well!"

She raised an eyebrow. "Not as well as you wish to be. It obviously pained you a great deal when you bowed just now. And should you let go of that chair, I think it very likely you would end up on the floor."

"And you being here is tiring him even more," said Lady Matlock, shamelessly pouncing on Elizabeth's observations. "We thank you for coming, but it will be for the best if you leave now."

Darcy tried to shake his head but something beneath his bandages pulled taut, and he winced in pain. Elizabeth mistook it for something else, though, for her face fell, and after earnestly but succinctly wishing him good health and happiness, she turned to go.

"*No! Do not leave!*" Darcy mouthed, but she was walking towards the door and did not see.

"What reason has she to stay, Darcy?" said Ladbroke under his breath. "She came to see how you are, she has seen, now she can go. There really is no need for you ever to see her again."

So began a trickle of voices that soon rose to a cacophony of opinions seemingly designed to chase Elizabeth from his life.

"Would you be good enough to take us home, Mr Bingley?"

"I think that would be for the best."

"There is no need to call again, Miss Bennet. He will be well taken care of."

"Go to bed, Darcy. We will admit no more nuisance callers."

Darcy banged his fist on the table so hard it jumped sideways. The room fell silent and all eyes turned to him, including Elizabeth's, upon which he fixed his own. "*Pray, do not leave on account of my family. They do not speak for me,*" he mouthed.

She shook her head and looked unbearably sad. "Mr Darcy, that situation is no different than you have ever given me reason to expect—and I am sorry to say, it does not trouble me half as much as I am sure it ought to. It is not their opinion of me I care about."

She began to turn away again, and Darcy felt a greater panic at the prospect of losing her than ever he had felt at not being able to draw breath into his lungs. He filled them now, to their very limit, and half forced, half choked the air out as he compelled himself to speak. "Then stay because I love you!"

A collective gasp sucked all the air from the room, and for a brief moment, Elizabeth and he were the only ones in it, staring at each other on the precipice of something yet to be defined. Then the vacuum burst, and sound rushed back in as an uproar of celebrations and remonstrations erupted around them. Fitzwilliam slapped him on the shoulder, jarring his neck, and congratulated him on the return of his voice—sentiments echoed by Bingley. Georgiana burst into tears. Lady Matlock declared he must still be feverish, instructed everybody to ignore his delirious raptures, and ordered him to bed. Lady Catherine railed in outrage at his betrayal, her daughter's disappointed hopes, and the whole family's certain ruin. Lord Matlock groaned. Ladbroke laughed.

It all sank to nothing in Darcy's awareness. He looked only at Elizabeth, who stared back at him, wide-eyed and, in contrast to everybody else, conspicuously silent. Fortified by trepidation and hope in equal measure, he approached her and took both her hands in his. His second attempt to speak produced nothing more than a painful rasp, but he had no qualms in reverting to mute speech, confident he would be understood. "*I love you, Elizabeth. I have been in love with you for a very long time, but never have I felt it more deeply than during our time together this week."*

"What is it you are saying, Darcy? What are you telling Miss Bennet? Let me hear what it is," Lady Catherine demanded.

Darcy ignored her, detesting that anybody should obtrude upon this moment, but too afraid of letting Elizabeth leave before she comprehended his feelings to delay it. *"You saved me in more ways than one. You taught me what I need to do and who I need to become to be worthy of you. I beg you would allow me that honour. Elizabeth, will you make me the happiest of men and consent to be my wife?"*

He waited in wretched suspense for her to answer, but rather than speak, she pulled her hands from his. His heart contracted painfully as he watched them withdraw. Then it faltered and began to race as she slowly but very deliberately touched the finger of one hand to the back of her other. He looked up to encounter her eyes and discovered her face diffused with heartfelt delight to match that which threatened to overwhelm him. He reclaimed both her hands and brought them to his lips. *"Thank you."*

The hue and cry around them grew positively feverish as everybody present conjectured, exclaimed, or ranted at what they supposed had transpired under their noses. Elizabeth said not a word, only squeezed Darcy's hands in return and smiled joyfully, and he felt the very great compliment of his declaration having rendered his usually vivacious and witty beloved utterly and completely speechless.

Of One Mind

Darcy kicked the door closed behind him, tugged Elizabeth's hand to turn her back towards him, and pulled her close. Still she said not a word, but as he watched, the look that had decided his heart at the inn returned to her countenance. Her lips parted, her eyes darkened, and she gave the tiniest gasp—an almost inaudible inhalation that spoke volumes as to her anticipation.

He answered the invitation. Taking her face in both his hands, he lowered his lips to hers. His neck screamed for him to desist, but other, more demanding urges begged him not to. He kissed her, and every blank his imagination had attempted to fill these past ten days took form beneath his hands. No longer must he wonder at the tenderness of her lips or the delicacy of her skin. Now he *knew* the softness of the curls at the nape of her neck, the depth of the hollow at the small of her back, the sweep of her hips that perfectly matched the curve of his palms, and the devastating power of her caress.

"What you do to me, Elizabeth!" he mouthed, pulling away slightly and resting his forehead upon hers. She returned his gaze affectionately, biting her lips as though still able to taste him there. Words seemed to have completely failed her, but he cared not, for she had left him in no doubt of her feelings.

Raised voices erupted on the other side of the door. Hardly surprising—he had, with several discreet but not particularly civil hand gestures, asked Fitzwilliam to escort everybody but Bingley, Georgiana, and Mrs Gardiner from the house while he stole this private moment with his newly betrothed. It sounded as though he would owe his cousin several cases of exceedingly expensive wine for his troubles. He rolled his eyes, drawing a small huff of laughter from Elizabeth.

"Will they ever forgive you, do you think?" she said softly, finding her voice at last.

He dared the discomfort of a shrug and mouthed, "*After the way they behaved towards you and your aunt, I hardly care.*" He surprised himself with a smile as he reflected on the scene—Elizabeth's influence, he was sure, for he would never usually have seen anything amusing in it. "*It was not the way I would have chosen to make my addresses.*"

She returned his grin. "You certainly succeeded in amazing the whole room."

It lifted his heart to be the object of her teasing having come so close to never hearing it again. "*I am sorry you were amazed. Would that I had done more to show you how I felt.*"

"I blinded myself to it, I am sure," she replied with a shake of her head. "I thought you disdained me in Hertfordshire and had no reason to think that had changed when I saw you again. Even when you began calling me Elizabeth—"

"*I did?*"

She smirked. "Aye. I just assumed it was easier for you to say."

He laughed a little at himself at having done such a thing unconsciously. It hurt his throat and reminded him of that fatigue which happiness had allowed him briefly to forget. He led Elizabeth to his desk, where he pulled a second chair close to his own for them to sit next to each other and resumed the conversation on paper.

> *It was my pride, my unjustifiable conceit, that prevented you from knowing my feelings. I worked hard to repress them until you showed me the absurdity of all my prepossessions. When I realised that I had actually made you hate me, I—*

"Hate you!" Elizabeth interrupted. "I thought you were disagreeable and proud when I first knew you, it is true, but it was not long after you woke up at the inn that I began to realise I was mistaken. After that, my opinion of you improved with almost every conversation. By the evening of the last day, I… well, I dearly wished to believe you when you declared yourself."

Darcy frowned in puzzlement, and she broke into a beatific smile, laughing as she exclaimed, "So I *was* right not to believe it! You *were* delirious!"

"*Believe what?*"

"You told me I had utterly bewitched you."

He shook his head slightly as he dipped his pen, mindful of his stitches but nonetheless incredulous. What a thing to forget!

> *I confess, I do not recall saying it, but I beg you would believe it. Never has a truer word been spoken.*

On reflection, he crossed out the word *spoken* and replaced it with *mouthed*. Elizabeth did not reply but leant forward in her chair, took the pen from his fingers, and wrote,

> *Mouthed or spoken, I treasure the sentiment.*

Darcy reached to take the pen back to reply, but she snatched it away playfully and added to her note.

> *I am very happy your voice has returned, though, for I like it very well. Nobody talks to me the way you do. You debate with me — as your equal.*

He opened the nearest drawer and took out a different pen, which he dipped in the ink and replied,

> *Elizabeth, you are my superior in every way.*

With a look of challenge, she shuffled her chair nearer to the desk.

> *A second pen is cheating, sir, and you are wrong in the other regard as well. In impertinence — and perhaps in nursing injured Samaritans — I suppose I might claim the upper hand, but you have proved yourself better than I at many other things.*

"*Name one,*" he mouthed defiantly. Her countenance assumed a devilish quality that drew Darcy forward to read what she would write.

> *I shall not name it, but I cannot pretend to rival the proficiency with which you have demonstrated your affections in the last few minutes.*

This answer might have convinced Darcy he was still delusional had the pleasure it produced not been far greater than any he could have conceived himself. He leant on the desk, his arm lying alongside Elizabeth's as he wrote,

> *I noticed no deficiency.*
> *Name another.*

Her lips quirked and Darcy felt an echoing twitch somewhere inside him that he did his best to ignore, for Elizabeth seemed to grow more serious as she dipped her pen to reply.

> *You are braver than I am. I should never have been as self-possessed with so serious an injury.*

He extended a forefinger to contradict her.

You could not be more wrong; I have never been more frightened in my life. The
only thing that prevented me from losing my composure was you.
Whereas you are fearless. Not even Lady Catherine's scorn could scare you.

She laughed. "Your aunt thinks me an insolent creature, I am sure, but there is a stubbornness about me that never can bear to be frightened at the will of others." Her smile faded a little. She put down her pen and turned to face him more fully. "I am in earnest though, Darcy. There *are* some things in which I am deficient, and I must be allowed to own them, as you have. You are not the only one to have been taught a lesson this past week. In questioning you so *ruthlessly*, I learnt many things about myself, few of them good, and I fear I was a far less gracious student than you."

Darcy opened his mouth to reply, but Elizabeth forestalled him with a hand on his arm and an extraordinary look that was at once ardent and grave. "You have shared so much with me. I have come to know you better than almost anyone of my acquaintance and…" She paused, looking down at her hand briefly, but continued after a self-conscious smile and shaky breath. "And though your feelings are of longer duration, I do not believe they are felt any less deeply than my own. You are not alone in emerging from this experience very much in love."

Elation swelled Darcy's heart until it pressed painfully against his ribs. His smile felt unfamiliar, broadened by happiness beyond his usual reserve. He lifted a hand to cradle her head, his fingers in her hair and his thumb stroking her cheek. "Dearest, loveliest Elizabeth." His voice was hoarse and weak, but he spoke aloud, and the words were as soothing to his throat as were her affections to his heart—and her kiss to his lips.

Arts, Allurements and Affiances

Darcy arrived with his sister at Grosvenor Street earlier than the invitation specified, but a week of confinement had left him impatient for escape. His wound was healing well, his strength and appetite returned. The only remaining complaint was that his voice was no more improved, and Farnham had advised him not to attempt to use it yet, to avoid doing further damage. It mattered not, for Elizabeth would be able to interpret for him, and she was due to arrive with her aunt, uncle, father, and sister within the next quarter of an hour.

"Darcy, Miss Darcy! You are very welcome!" Bingley greeted them with more than his usual effusiveness at the front door, unceremoniously barging past the footman and opening his arms wide. To Darcy in particular, he said, "You look much more like yourself, old fruit! Come in, come in! I've a new tipple on the go that is really only safe for you, for it is guaranteed to blister the voice box clean off anyone else who tries it. Come in!"

Darcy smiled at Bingley's effervescent manner, which was unquestionably a consequence of his recent engagement to Elizabeth's older sister. Upon learning of Jane's enduring affections, his friend had left posthaste for Hertfordshire to recommence his pursuit of her hand. Once there, he seemed to have taken his lead from Darcy's example and, with the omission of a near-fatal blow to the neck, had constrained his efforts to one week and an impetuous plea for her hand. To London the pair had returned, ostensibly to share the news with him and Elizabeth, who had refused to return home whilst he was yet too unwell to travel. Darcy suspected, however, that in truth the trip had been conceived as a means to evade Mrs Bennet's raptures.

Bingley's siblings awaited them in the drawing room. Mr and Mrs Hurst welcomed them cordially; Miss Bingley came forward to grasp both Georgiana's hands in a show of intimacy by which his sister was evidently bemused. "Good evening, Miss Darcy, what a joy to see you again after so long. And Mr Darcy! How delighted we all are that you are well enough to join us. It is wonderful to see you looking so well after such a dreadful ordeal."

Darcy bowed, unable to recall when it had last been necessary for him bite the insides of his cheeks to keep a straight face. He wished Elizabeth had been less eloquent on the subject of Miss Bingley's officious attentions. He wondered whether his engagement would temper the lady's manner at all but was resigned to being overly aware of it all evening either way.

Miss Bingley's smile faltered when he did not reply, and she looked uneasily at her brother.

"He cannot speak, Caroline. You know this," Bingley said to her. "And believe me when I say it is easiest for him not to bother trying to make himself understood by mouthing anything. It is a tortuous process."

"*For a man with the patience of a flea, perhaps,*" Darcy retorted mutely.

Miss Bingley gave a prim little laugh. "Mr Darcy's words may be indecipherable, Charles, but I can understand that look well enough. I forbid you from teasing him any further."

"Fear not, Caroline," said Hurst. "Miss Bennet will be here soon, and then your brother will have no time for anybody else, to tease them or otherwise."

"But then Lizzy will be here, too, and she will tease him enough for all of us."

Everybody, Darcy included, looked at Georgiana in surprise. Seldom was she brave enough to speak so boldly in company, and even more rarely was she sportive. It truly was astonishing what alterations Elizabeth could bring about in people in the space of but one week.

"Teases him, does she?" Hurst said with a grin. "How the mighty have fallen." Darcy treated him to a look of a different sort, whereupon he stopped grinning and sat back down with a grunt.

The sound of a carriage pulling up outside saw Bingley capering back to the front door, drawing the mockery they had all been forbidden from directing at Darcy. Darcy observed good manners and waited where he was for the Bennets and the Gardiners to be shown in, his own boyish flurry of anticipation locked securely behind a carefully neutral expression. His equanimity was severely tested when Elizabeth came in, resplendent in full evening dress, and sought out his gaze before any other. He dared permit himself only a small smile. Any more and he risked making himself ridiculous with an inane grin.

"*You look divine,*" he mouthed to her when they came together, he taking her hands in his and kissing them.

"Thank you," she replied. "How are you feeling? It is not too much to be out and about?"

He shook his head—a recently regained ability. *"It is a relief to be out of the house."*

Her eyes shone. "Jane and Papa have both expressed similar sentiments."

As he suspected, then. *"You are pleased to see them?"*

"Exceedingly so, though it did deprive me of *your* company all day. I have grown used to our being constantly together."

Darcy fancied he was far more conscious than Elizabeth of the times they were apart, those generally being the nocturnal hours, when he was most impatient for them to be together. *"I missed you, too,"* he mouthed, *"Though my meeting with your father went well."*

"Yes, so he told me. I believe he appreciated your frankness."

Darcy rather thought it was the figure he had written down in answer to the question of whether he had sufficient means to support Elizabeth that Bennet had appreciated. Both men had been silent after that, the alliance settled with a wordless shake of hands. *"Speaking of frankness, I had a letter today. From Lady Catherine."*

"Oh. I suppose it was not overflowing with congratulations."

The letter had indeed been overflowing, but with language so abusive, especially of Elizabeth, that Darcy had, against the physician's orders, voiced a string of invective that left his throat raw. *"No."*

Elizabeth laid a hand on his arm and squeezed gently—then raised her eyebrows and said impishly, "She will not be coming for Christmas then?"

Darcy prevented himself from laughing fully aloud but still wheezed noisily and unevenly. Always, her wit took him unawares. The hiatus in their conversation left the room notably quiet. He glanced sidelong at the other occupants, then back at Elizabeth with a smirk. She did the same, then bit her lips together in amusement. Everybody present was staring at them with varying degrees of fascination, perplexity, and amusement.

"It is extraordinary, is it not?" Mrs Gardiner remarked. "They have been doing that all week. It is impossible to follow."

"I am not surprised by it," Mr Bennet said. "I can barely get a word in edgeways *with* a voice. Without one, Mr Darcy stands no chance."

"I daresay you will have more opportunity to be heard when these two are no longer at home," Mr Gardiner said, indicating his nieces with a nod.

"With Lizzy gone, perhaps," Mr Bennet replied with a twinkle in his eye. "Jane has never been as much trouble."

Elizabeth laughed. "Why, thank you, Papa, but though the comparison *has* been drawn"—she glanced at Darcy—"even I am not as spirited as Lydia. You will have to wait for her to marry before you truly have any peace at Longbourn."

"And you may rest assured that will not be for *many* years," her father replied, also glancing at Darcy and giving him a small nod, "therefore you may expect me to visit Pemberley very often to escape the noise at home."

Darcy returned the nod with a small one of his own. Since even Elizabeth had been so thoroughly taken in, he had made sure to warn Mr Bennet against allowing any of his other, less sensible daughters to befriend Wickham. A few extra visits were something to which he would gladly submit if it would avoid any of his new sisters being embroiled in scandal. Indeed, perceiving the similarity between Elizabeth's playfulness and her father's—something he had not appreciated before this evening—made the prospect of his visiting even less onerous.

"*You are welcome at any time, sir,*" he mouthed.

Mr Bennet raised his eyebrows and turned his head slightly, as though expecting that the words might yet to find their way to his ears if he listened hard enough.

"He said you are welcome occasionally, and only if you do not bring the noise with you," Elizabeth said, which was much closer to what Darcy had meant.

ELIZABETH'S PARAPHRASING HIS COMMENTS BECAME SOMETHING OF A THEME FOR the remainder of the evening. Those who knew Darcy best of the company grew increasingly perplexed by the answers Elizabeth occasionally put in his mouth. Those who knew her best seemed better able take everything she said with a pinch of salt and only shook their heads and smiled secretly at their dinner plates. At some point towards the end of dinner, however, somewhere after his third glass of wine, it happened that the tables turned, and Elizabeth found it necessary to begin moderating *his* remarks.

"I hope you like the gammon, Mr Darcy," Miss Bingley said around the footman refilling her glass. "I had cook prepare it especially for you. I thought you might enjoy a treat after having been indisposed for so long, and I know it is your favourite."

Darcy did not miss the sly glance she sent to Elizabeth as she said this. He was certain Elizabeth saw it too, though she was good enough to pretend she had not. "Is it?" she enquired innocently instead.

"*It is,*" he admitted.

"Really, Miss Eliza," Miss Bingley exclaimed. "Do you not even know which are your future husband's favourite foods?"

Elizabeth maintained her easy smile. "Not yet, Miss Bingley. We did not have much opportunity at the inn to experiment with different menus. Besides, I am not sure how well Mr Darcy would have got on with gammon, given that he could barely swallow a spoonful of water at the beginning of the week."

Darcy was not getting on with it much better at present and was having to cut his food into infinitesimal pieces and smother it in gravy to keep from choking on every mouthful. Hardly the most thoughtful of meals to serve up in the circumstances. "*I am fast going off it,*" he mouthed, looking disdainfully at the slab of meat on his plate. "*Was it absolutely necessary for the cook to desic-cate the pig before he cooked it?*"

"Pardon?" Miss Bingley enquired.

Elizabeth dabbed her lips with a napkin, holding it to her mouth until her smile was gone before translating. "He said it is taking a while to get used to eating solid food again."

"I should stick to liquids, Darcy," Hurst suggested, raising his glass. "Far better for the constitution."

"What *did* you eat, Lizzy?" Georgiana enquired.

"Mostly bread, cheese, and cured meats. There was a little fruit at the beginning, but that soon ran out. There was a veritable cornucopia of onions and potatoes in the cellar, though. If I never eat another of either, it will not be too soon."

Darcy was diverted to note that she had, indeed, eschewed dishing any potatoes onto her plate and had picked all the onions out of the ragout.

"I thought you said you could not eat solids, Darcy," Bingley said, frowning.

To which he, running short of patience, replied, "*Georgiana asked what Eliza-beth ate, not I. I dined on brandy, broth, and thin air for the most part.*"

"Brandy and what?"

"Broth," Elizabeth summarised. "Which, by the end of the week, I had perfected to a finely tuned balance of salty water and boiled onions. Your cook would be in awe, Miss Bingley."

"*You* cooked his meals?" Bingley said admiringly.

When Elizabeth acknowledged this was true, Miss Bingley, less admiringly, enquired, "How on earth do you know how to cook, Miss Eliza?"

"Yes, Lizzy," said her sister. "How *do* you know how to cook?"

"I am not sure Mr Darcy would agree that I can, but there was a soldier at the inn who had some knowledge of campfire cooking. From him, I learnt the general principle that boiling things in water will flavour it. That is as far as my abilities extend, I am afraid."

"*Boiling things in water also adds moisture,*" Darcy mouthed. "*I daresay you could teach Bingley's cook a thing or two.*"

"What was that, Darcy?"

Observably struggling to keep her countenance, Elizabeth sent him a look of half-laughing admonishment that begged him to desist. "At least I shall not be called upon to cook at Pemberley. I understand from Miss Darcy the cook there is wonderful."

"He is," Hurst agreed. "The very best."

"I tried to poach him once," Bingley said with a grin. "Do you remember, Darcy?"

Darcy nodded.

"Charles!" Jane exclaimed. "How ungallant!"

"Pish posh, Jane—you would have thanked me had I succeeded. He makes the best bread pudding this side of East Riding. And in any case, I never would have attempted it had Darcy not poached my footman the week before."

Darcy regarded him incredulously. *"You let him go because you forgot you had a lock fitted and thought he had barred you from your own house. I gave him work at your behest because you felt guilty."*

"What is he saying, Lizzy?" Bingley enquired. "You must not believe half of what he says, you know. He is a good deal too apt to be overly serious about these things."

"I might have believed that a month ago," Elizabeth replied, looking between them with delight. "But you will no longer convince me of any such thing."

"I think it is time we ladies withdrew," Miss Bingley announced curtly. "Cambridge, clear the table please."

"What say we forego separating this evening, Caroline?" said Bingley. "There seems little point in subjecting Darcy to half an hour of being asked to repeat himself, for none of us can understand him without Lizzy to translate."

"I am not at all sure we have understood him *with* Lizzy's help," Mr Gardiner said. "I do believe she has been making it up as she has gone along."

"Uncle! How could you say such a thing?" Elizabeth replied with affected affront.

Nonetheless, it was decided that the gentlemen and the ladies would adjourn together. As they left the room, Darcy caught hold of Elizabeth's hand and pulled her away from the rest of the party. There were no candles lit in the alcove to which he led her, and he was forced to whisper rather than mouth what he wished to say.

"I love you, Elizabeth."

"Oh no, Darcy, stop!" she replied in a quiet but urgent voice. "You are not to use your voice."

"Very well," he croaked and kissed her, fleetingly but passionately, instead.

She gasped and whirled about looking for witnesses, of which he had been assured there were none before he acted. Satisfied of the same, she let out a breath and whispered, "You have the devil in you this evening, sir."

"Are you displeased?"

There was a pause—then, "No."

He was glad of the dark, for if his expression came anywhere close to matching his thoughts, it might make him appear more rakish than he would like. "You were right about Miss Bingley," he said, his voice growing hoarser with every word.

"Actually," Elizabeth replied, "I am inclined to think *you* were right. She made the odd sortie, I know, but it cannot have been easy to host us this evening, knowing everybody was aware of her hopes where you were concerned. I thought she was very dignified considering."

Darcy felt for her shoulders, smoothed his hands down over her upper arms, and pressed a gentle kiss to her forehead. "It is *your* dignity and forbearance that allowed her to appear in such a good light." He had said too much; his voice cracked, and he coughed painfully.

Elizabeth placed her hand upon his right cheek and kissed him on his left. "It is *your* forbearance that ever allowed me to know you well enough to make Miss Bingley jealous." Then she proved the devil was every bit as much in her by kissing him full on the lips.

His having coughed so loudly beforehand proved to be a most convenient excuse for their delayed return to the drawing room, as well as the discomposure that returned him, for the remainder of the evening, to the sombre creature that had stalked the walls of Meryton's ballrooms last autumn, attempting not to be overwhelmed by Elizabeth's Bennet's charms.

No Need of Words

Darcy knew they must be at the spot, or nearing it, when Elizabeth tensed at his side. He looked out of the window at the passing scenery but felt no peculiar uneasiness. It was merely a wooded road with nothing to suggest it had been the scene of one man's death, another's narrow escape, and the source of all his present and future happiness. He remembered nothing of the accident to this day and was more than content that he never should.

"It is well, Elizabeth. There is nothing here but clear road."

"I know, only I do not like to think of it. Poor Mr Perkins. And you, lying in the snow like that." She shuddered a little.

"Given your ill opinion of me at the time, I am almost afraid of asking what you thought when you discovered it *was* me lying in the snow."

"Oh, I knew it was you before that. I recognised you as soon as you rode into view. But I did not have much time to think about it in that moment. It was all too immediate. It was only after Rogers and I got you to the inn, and the snow began to get deeper, and I realised we were stuck there that I…"

"You were angry?"

"No—at least, not with you. How could I be when you had only tried to help? But I was angry with the world for throwing us together. It felt as though Fate was playing a very cruel trick." Her mouth twisted into a wry smile. "Of course, I did not know then that you had all but thrown yourself into my path with your reckless jaunt through a snowstorm to look for me. Had I been aware of *that*, I might have been angrier with you."

"I found you, did I not?"

"You certainly did! But now you must tell me, for your remark rather begs the question, were *you* angry when you realised I was tending to you?"

Darcy chuckled a little. "I was absolutely furious—once I regained enough wits to comprehend that you were not a figment of my imagination." In answer to her querying look, he added, "It would not have been the first time I had dreamt of you."

She coloured slightly at the compliment, though her eyes revealed her amusement at his confession. It was a powerful combination—too powerful to resist. He lifted her chin with a finger and kissed her. He would have stopped at that, had she not returned his caress with such fervour. Then, before he knew it, her hands were tangled in his hair, his hands were exploring the different shape of her when she was folded into a carriage seat, and his ardour had risen to a point from which it was exceedingly difficult to return.

"There were more times than I could count while we were in that place that I wished to do that," he said with heavy breath when they parted.

"There were quite a few times *I* wished you would do that," she replied. "Do not look so surprised. I have eyes, sir—and warm blood."

Darcy did not correct her. It would not be long before Elizabeth learnt it was not *surprise* remarks such as that provoked. "As do I. You have no idea the agonies I suffered at your hands. I had to pretend complete indifference every time you touched me, every time you knelt on the bed or lifted my head. And you know now that *indifferent* is very far from what I truly felt. I even enjoyed it when you cut my face."

She huffed a small laugh and tipped her head up to kiss the place where the small scratch had long since healed. "I suppose necessity did rather oblige us to dispense with all the usual awkwardness of falling in love. I cannot say I am sorry. I do not think Jane and Bingley are as easy with each other yet."

"They very soon will be."

She bit her lip. "Yes, that is true. They seemed very happy today, did they not?"

"I could not say. I paid no attention to anybody but you."

That earned him a broad smile. "Then you must take my word for it. Jane looked beautiful, as Jane always does, and Bingley was the happiest I have ever seen him."

Darcy ran the knuckle of one finger along her jaw to her chin, then ran his thumb along her lower lip. "*You* looked beautiful, Elizabeth. As *you* always do." He kissed her again, half marvelling, half ruing how far she must have gone to find help after the accident, for he was more than ready to arrive at their destination.

"Are we almost there, do you think?" Elizabeth enquired.

Her thoughts so closely mirrored his own that he laughed, though the suddenness caught in his throat, as it often did still, and he coughed. "You tell me, you are the only one to have walked it."

Her expression lost its urgency and softened into one of concern. "You are losing your voice again."

"Hardly surprising. I have done much talking today."

Elizabeth rummaged in her reticule for the hip flask she had charmed off her uncle in London and taken to carrying with honeyed water for Darcy to drink whenever his voice grew hoarse. "Thank you for talking to my mother for so long," she said as she passed it to him. "I believe she is a little in awe of you, else she might have gone on even longer, but still, you bore it with extraordinary civility."

"She may thank you for that. You taught me to appreciate her good qualities." He dabbed his lips dry with his cuff and passed the flask back. His voice was not less gravelly, but his throat hurt less. "I comprehend that she was merely relieved to have two fewer people about whose futures she need be anxious."

"If only that meant her effusions would be lessened by two fifths rather than transferred in undiminished magnitude to my other poor sisters. You are very wise to have overlooked her transports about your fortune, though. It would only recall you to the argument she had with my Aunt Philips about who tailors your clothes, and that would inevitably remind you of the little soliloquy she gave to the whole party about your looks."

"Hmm. I shall not deny that had I been in the country as long as Bingley, I might not have been quite so forbearing. He has been here for most of the time that you and I have been in Town, and I fear even his good humour has worn thin."

She winced. "Poor Mama. She means well but is incapable of passing up any opportunity to be vulgar that presents itself."

"At least she *does* mean well," Darcy replied, feeling rather guilty, for he was in no position to censure Elizabeth's relations. "Lady Catherine, on the other hand, has made it her business to offend you by every possible method. Compared to her behaviour, your mother's occasional impropriety is entirely forgivable."

Elizabeth rubbed his forearm, her brows drawn together in sympathy. "Not all your relations are so determined to despise me. Your cousins seemed to enjoy themselves today—and do not try to tell me they came only to take Georgiana home, for it would not have taken both of them to do that. One of them at least must have come of his own free will."

"Granted." He picked up her hand and pulled her glove off, finger by finger. "Anne did not come."

"That was a vain hope. Was it not enough to have Miss Bingley there? Did you need every woman who ever set her cap at you at your wedding?"

He smiled, savouring her teasing, and lifted her hand to his lips to kiss her palm. "I am merely demonstrating that I have more relations who have treated you with contempt than the reverse." He moved his lips to her wrist.

"Lady Matlock does not despise me."

"Not now that you are her ticket to every fashionable soiree in London." His aunt had begun, at Fitzwilliam's urging, by condescending to take Elizabeth shopping. After the third lady of the *ton* had stopped them to enquire about the accident, Lady Matlock had recognised the value of her new niece and forbidden her from answering any further questions unless under the explicit invitation of one of a dozen particular ladies and, even then, only once inside their front doors. Elizabeth had confessed to being vastly diverted by the whole thing, and—judging by the questions Darcy was occasionally asked when he was out—she had not scrupled in embellishing the story in ever more ludicrous ways, no doubt for some mischievous reason of her own.

He tugged her gently towards him and kissed her neck. "Of all the intrigues to have enthralled London that I can recall, you are by far my favourite." They were poised to kiss, the jouncing carriage jostling them so that sometimes their lips were touching and sometimes they were not, when the driver banged on the roof and shouted that they had arrived. Darcy would have kissed Elizabeth anyway had she not been startled into laughing at herself.

"Good gracious, does he always do that? I think I just aged ten years!"

Darcy smiled a deliberately suggestive smile. "No, but he does not usually have such good reason to suspect I may not be paying attention to my journey." He enjoyed the blush that crept up Elizabeth's neck as he handed her down from the carriage and turned her towards the front door. They had gone only a few steps in that direction when it was flung open and a young man strode towards them, calling over his shoulder as he did.

"Uncle, they are here!"

Another figure appeared in the doorway and walked lopsidedly towards them. "What's that, John? Are they here? Is it Mr and Mrs Darcy?"

Elizabeth glanced at Darcy with a private, triumphant smile before calling back, "Yes, Mr Timmins. It is."

"You are very well met. How good it is to see you both again. And you looking so well, Mr Darcy."

"Thank you, sir. It is excellent to see you again."

"Ah! So that is what you sound like."

"Actually, it is not really," Elizabeth said, wrinkling her nose in pity. "My husband has been talking all day, and his voice is not yet fully recovered and still easily lost."

"That is most unfortunate," Mr Timmins replied.

Darcy was inclined to think otherwise. He had said his vows; those were the only words that needed to be spoken aloud today. He was assured that the performance of none of his other duties as a newly wedded husband would be hindered by the loss of his voice. "We shall get by," he said benignly.

"I doubt it not, for you did before. I recall it well, sir. As well-attuned a couple as ever I saw."

Elizabeth enjoyed that compliment, Darcy could tell, for her smile widened, her eyes glittered, and she rewarded the innkeeper with a little flattery of her own. "Mr Timmins, I cannot express how lovely this place is when it is not buried under three feet of snow. All these daffodils, that little stream that I never even knew was there…it is like a fairy tale."

Timmins beamed. "I think you will like the inside better than on your last visit as well, Mrs Darcy. We have prepared the best room for you this time."

Darcy had made certain of that. In an exchange of several letters during his convalescence, he had first thanked and repaid Timmins for his assistance, then enlightened him as to the identity and consequence of his erstwhile guest, then arranged lodgings for this particular day, then forwarded a mutually agreed sum for the renovation of the inn in readiness for the arrival, in all their state, of Mr and Mrs Darcy of Pemberley. It was money with which he had been more than happy to part, for the Dancing Bear was not only the place where he and Elizabeth had been finally united; it was also the place his life had been saved. Had the accident happened any farther away, had Timmins not opened his doors to them, Darcy would almost certainly have died several miles back on the side of the road.

"Oh, you have moved Mr Collins."

"At your suggestion, Mrs Darcy, at your suggestion," Timmins replied. "You were right. No use naming an inn after him then hiding him at the bottom of the stairs."

Darcy looked around. They had come inside the inn, and the only difference that he could perceive in this room was that the great stuffed bear had been brought to stand by the front door. He gestured to it. "Mr Collins?"

Elizabeth grinned. "I named him when we were here last. There is a likeness, do you not agree? My cousin is such a tall, heavy-looking man. And strangely hirsute."

Darcy rolled his eyes and tried not to be as amused as he was.

"Lizzy! Mr Darcy! How absolutely wonderful to see you!"

Darcy watched Elizabeth for her response as a lady rose from one of the tables and came towards them. Her smile as she recognised Mrs Stratton, then, glancing around the room, Mr Stratton, Mr and Mrs Ormerod, and Lieutenant Carver, satisfied him that the surprise had been well judged.

"And you! All of you," Elizabeth replied happily. Turning to Darcy, she began to say something, then stopped and peered at him more closely. "You do not seem surprised. Did you arrange this?"

He shrugged. "There is no private dining room here. I thought, if we must dine with company, we might as well guarantee it is superior company."

"Well said, sir," Timmins said jovially. "It will be with superior food as well, for your cook has been working since before dawn, preparing a feast fit for kings."

Elizabeth looked at Darcy.

"I sent for him from Pemberley," he explained.

"You have excelled yourself, sir," Elizabeth said, with a look so exceedingly warm it made Darcy wish he had not arranged any of it, for he would much rather take her directly above stairs than remain here and eat, no matter how agreeable the company or the food. Still, at only four o'clock in the afternoon, he could scarcely justify such behaviour, and thus downstairs they remained.

By the end of the evening, Darcy was prodigiously pleased they had, for he would be hard pressed to recall a more enjoyable gathering. Edouard had outdone himself in the kitchen. The wine, a gift from Mr Gardiner's warehouse, was better than many Darcy had tasted on the continent. Their party, increased by one as they were joined by Timmins's sister, Mrs Dreyford, was on excellent form. Elizabeth was in her element: gracious, teasing, and, to his own unqualified pleasure, obviously delighted.

Dinner ended with a toast. He and Elizabeth had already expressed their thanks to every person present with letters of gratitude, as well as an ornate new inkwell for Mrs Ormerod, an exquisite new gown for Mrs Stratton, a far superior bottle of brandy for Timmins than the one he had allowed Elizabeth to pour over and down Darcy's neck, and finely tailored shirts to replace those donated by Mr Ormerod and Lieutenant Carver. Nonetheless, they raised their glasses and expressed their deepest thanks once again.

"Thank *you*, dearest Fitzwilliam," Elizabeth whispered to Darcy. "I could not have conceived of a better way to celebrate getting married."

"Getting married?" said Mrs Dreyford said on Elizabeth's other side. "I beg your pardon, Mrs Darcy. I understood from my brother that you were already married. I would have congratulated you sooner had I realised."

Elizabeth opened and closed her mouth several times without articulating an actual response. Her discomfiture was justified; *everybody* here was under the impression they had been married for some time and that today's celebrations were a means of thanking them all for their part in saving Darcy's life. It would be unfortunate were the truth of the matter to be revealed at this late stage.

"Mrs Darcy's sister was married in Meryton this morning, madam," Darcy said, glad that truth would add weight to the tale and even gladder when Elizabeth squeezed his knee under the table by way of thanks.

"Oh, I see," Mrs Dreyford replied. "You have had quite a day of celebrations then!"

"Indeed we have," Elizabeth agreed. "We always planned to stay here on our way home from the wedding, for it was to be first time we returned to the area since the accident. I did not know any of you would be here, though. Mr Darcy kept that as a surprise."

"Well, I hope your sister has had as pleasant an evening as we all have."

"*I* hope she and her new husband do not have too far to travel to their new home," Timmins interrupted. "Pardon me, Evie, I could not help but overhear," he added when his sister looked at him sharply.

"What relevance is the distance they must travel?" Stratton enquired as the conversation diffused throughout the rest of the party.

"I bet I can answer that," Carver offered, looking to Timmins for corroboration. "I bet you are thinking that it would be best for the new couple to avoid the same misfortune as Mr and Mrs Darcy have suffered on their travels."

"Fortunately, they do not have very far to go at all," Elizabeth replied. "Though I am sure they will do very well with whatever obstacles life throws in their path. They are both very good, very sensible, very sanguine people."

The conversation moved from there to which characters generally did best in times of trouble, with some lighthearted dispute over the advantages of bravery over forbearance.

"I daresay Bingley would make a far better patient than I if he were in the same position," Darcy said quietly to Elizabeth and meant it. "He is much better natured. He would have been far easier to appease and not half as apt to brood."

Elizabeth looked at him for a while before replying, her eyes gleaming with the smile to which her lips seemed reluctant to commit. "I daresay you are right about all those things," she said at length. "But he would not have been nearly so interesting a character to study. Dear though he is, I should have discovered everything there was to know about him in one afternoon and been numb with ennui for the rest of the week." She smiled then—a glorious, heart-felt smile that touched every part of her countenance and every hidden corner of Darcy's heart. "It will take me a lifetime to discover everything there is to know about you."

Darcy covered her hand with his and leant to whisper in her ear. "What good fortune, then, that a lifetime with me is what you have just agreed to, Mrs Darcy."

He excused them soon afterwards and took his bride upstairs. He was right: they required no words. They were both of them reverently silent as they resumed the study of each other they had begun the last time they were stranded here with only each other for company, and which Darcy fully intended should continue for the rest of his God-given life.

THE END

ACKNOWLEDGMENTS

Thank you, everybody at Quills and Quartos Publishing, for believing in me. And, as always, thank you Jane Austen, for the privilege of spending more time with your Darcy and Elizabeth, for the honour of incorporating some of your inimical writing into this alternative journey for them, and for inspiring me to write.

ABOUT THE AUTHOR

Jessie Lewis, author of *Mistaken* and *The Edification of Lady Susan*, enjoys words far too much for her own good and was forced to take up writing them down in order to save her family and friends from having to listen to her saying so many of them. She dabbled in poetry during her teenage years, though it was her studies in Literature and Philosophy at university that firmly established her admiration for the potency of the English language. She has always been particularly in awe of Jane Austen's literary cunning and has delighted in exploring Austen's regency world in her own historical fiction writing. It is of no relevance whatsoever to her ability to string words together coherently that she lives in Hertfordshire with two tame cats, two feral children and a pet husband. She is also quite tall, in case you were wondering.

You can check out her musings on the absurdities of language and life on her blog, **LifeinWords.blog**, or see what she's reading over at Goodreads. Or you can drop her a line on Twitter, @JessieWriter or on her Facebook page, Jessie-LewisAuthor.

To learn more about future releases from Jessie and other great historical fiction authors, please visit www.QuillsandQuartos.com

ALSO BY JESSIE LEWIS

Mistaken

Voted Austenesque Reviews Readers' Favourite 2017 and Austenesque Reviews Favourite 2018.

A tempestuous acquaintance and disastrous marriage proposal make it unlikely Mr Darcy and Elizabeth Bennet will ever reconcile. Despairing of their own reunion, they attend with great energy to salvaging that of Darcy's friend Mr Bingley and Elizabeth's sister Jane. People are rarely so easily manoeuvred in and out of love, however, and there follows a series of misunderstandings, both wilful and unwitting, that complicates the path to happiness for all four star-crossed lovers more than ever before.

A witty and romantic novel that delights in the folly of human nature, Mistaken both honours Jane Austen's original *Pride and Prejudice* and holds appeal for readers of all genres.

Rational Creatures: Stirrings of Feminism in the Hearts of Jane Austen's Fine Ladies (The Quill Collective Book 3)

Jane Austen: True romantic or rational creature? Her novels transport us back to the Regency, a time when well-mannered gentlemen and finely-bred ladies fell in love as they danced at balls and rode in carriages. Yet her heroines, such as Elizabeth Bennet, Anne Elliot, and Elinor Dashwood, were no swooning, fainthearted damsels in distress. Austen's novels have become timeless classics because of their biting wit, honest social commentary, and because she wrote of strong women who were ahead of their day. True to their principles and beliefs, they fought through hypocrisy and broke social boundaries to find their happily-ever-after.

In the third romance anthology of The Quill Collective series, sixteen celebrated Austenesque authors write the untold histories of Austen's brave adventuresses, her shy maidens, her talkative spinsters, and her naughty matrons. Peek around the curtain and discover what made Lady Susan so wicked, Mary Crawford so capricious, and Hettie Bates so in need of Emma Woodhouse's pity.

RATIONAL CREATURES is a collection of humorous, poignant, and engaging love stories set in Georgian England that complement and pay homage to Austen's great works and great ladies who were, perhaps, the first feminists in an era that was not quite ready for feminism. "Make women rational creatures, and free citizens, and they will become good wives; —that is, if men do not neglect the duties of husbands and fathers." —Mary Wollstonecraft

Stories by: Elizabeth Adams * Nicole Clarkston * Karen M Cox * J. Marie Croft * Amy D'Orazio * Jenetta James * Jessie Lewis * KaraLynne Mackrory * Lona Manning * Christina Morland * Beau North * Sophia Rose * Anngela Schroeder * Joana Starnes * Caitlin Williams * Edited by Christina Boyd * Foreword by Devoney Looser

Manufactured by Amazon.ca
Bolton, ON